350

MASCULINE PROTE

and other stories

Born in 1903, in Cork, Frank O'Co
his only real ambition was to become a w
to prepare a collected edition of his own works
speak Gaelic while very young, he studied his native
legends. His literary career began with the translation of
Bellay's sonnets into Gaelic.

On release from imprisonment by the Free State Government for his
part in the Civil War, O'Connor won a prize for his study of Turgenev
and subsequently had poetry, stories and translations published in the
Irish Statesman. He caused great consternation in his native city by
producing plays by Ibsen and Chekhov: a local clergyman remarked
that the producer 'would go down in posterity at the head of the pagan
Dublin muses', and ladies in the local literary society threatened to
resign when he mentioned the name of James Joyce. By profession
O'Connor was a librarian and his other great interest was music, Mozart
and the Irish composer Carolan being his favourites. He will long be
remembered for his collections of short stories. Frank O'Connor died
in March 1966.

A Life of Your Own and other stories, also available in Pan Books,
contains the balance of the stories originally published in
Collection Three

The cover photograph shows the
junction of Shandon Street and Pope's Quay, Cork

Frank O'Connor

MASCULINE PROTEST
and other stories from Collection Three

Pan Books in association with
Macmillan London

First published 1969 in *Collection Three* by Macmillan & Co Ltd
This edition (being the second part of the stories contained in
Collection Three except for 'The Martyr') published 1972 by
Pan Books Ltd, Cavaye Place, London SW10 9PG
in association with Macmillan London
3rd printing 1982
© Harriet O'Donovan 1952, 1954, 1955, 1957,
1958, 1959, 1967, 1968
ISBN 0 330 02984 3
Printed in Great Britain by
Cox & Wyman Ltd, Reading

CONTENTS

FOREWORD

FOR Frank O'Connor the most important single element in any story was its design. It might be years between the moment of recognizing a theme and finding the one right shape for it – this was the hard, painful work – the writing he did in his head. But once he had the essential bony structure firmly in place he could begin to enjoy the story – to start 'tinkering' with it. It was this 'tinkering' which produced dozens of versions of the same story. The basic design never changed, but in each new version light would be thrown in a different way on a different place. Frank O'Connor did this kind of rewriting endlessly – as he admits in the Introduction to *Collection Two*, he frequently continued it even after a story had been published. Though this confused and sometimes annoyed editors, reviewers and bibliographers, the multiplicity of versions was never a problem to him. When there were enough stories to form a new collection he didn't start trying to choose between the many extant versions of them – he simply sat down and prepared to rewrite every story he wanted in the book.

That particular rewriting was directed towards a definite aim – which was to give a book of stories the feeling of being a unity rather than a grab bag. He believed that stories – if arranged in an 'ideal ambience' – could strengthen and illuminate each other. This unity was only partly preconceived, he continued to create it as he went along. He never wrote a story specifically to fit into a gap in a book – nor did he change names or locations to give superficial unity. Rather it was as though the stories were bits of a mosaic which could be arranged harmoniously so that the pattern they made together reflected the light which each cast separately. Ultimately this unity probably sprang from his basic conviction that the writer was not simply an observer: 'I can't write about something I don't admire – it goes back to the old concept of the celebration: you celebrate the hero, an idea.'

This means, of course, that Frank O'Connor had very definite ideas about the contents and arrangements of each new book of stories. If he had lived, this might have been a different book. As it is, I have had to choose, not only which and how many stories to include, but also which of the many versions of each story to print. There was also the problem of that 'ideal ambience' and the comfort of the knowledge that even his own 'ideal ambience would be shattered by the time the book appears'.

I do not doubt that I shall have to answer to the author for each of these decisions. But for the stories themselves no one need answer. They are pure Frank O'Connor.

HARRIET O'DONOVAN (MRS FRANK O'CONNOR)

ACKNOWLEDGEMENTS

Acknowledgements are due to the following publications in which these stories first appeared: *Harper's Bazaar, John Bull, Mademoiselle, New Yorker, Penguin New Writing, Saturday Evening Post, Woman's Day*. The text of 'A Story by Maupassant', which first appeared in *Penguin New Writing* in 1945, is the completely revised version published in *Winter's Tales 14* in 1968.

MASCULINE PROTEST

FOR months things had been getting difficult between Mother and me. At the time we were living in Boharna, a small town twenty miles from the city – Father, Mother, Martha, and I. I had managed to put up with it by kidding myself that one day Mother would understand; one day she'd wake up and see that the affection of Dad and Martha was insincere, that the two had long ago ganged up against her, and that I, the black sheep, the clumsy, stupid Denis, was the only one who really loved her.

The revelation was due to take place in rather unusual circumstances. We were all to be stranded in some danger-ous desert, and Mother, with her ankle broken, would tell us to leave her to her fate. Dad and Martha would, of course, leave her, with only a pretence of concern. I could even imagine how Dad would look back regretfully, with his eye-brows raised, and shrug his shoulders, as much as to say that there was nothing he could do. But I, in my casual way, would simply fold my hands about my knees and ask list-lessly, 'What use is life to me without you? It's all very well for Dad and Martha; they have one another, but I have only you.' Not a word more! I was determined on not having any false drama, any raising of the voice. I was never one for high-flown expressions; the lift of the shoulder, the way I pulled a grass-blade to chew (it needn't be a desert), and Mother would realize that though I was not demon-strative – just a plain, rough, willing chap – I had a heart of gold.

But Mother had a genius for subjecting hearts of gold to intolerable strain. It was the same as with Flossie, our dog. We had been brought up with Flossie, but when Dad had to go on a long trip and Mother wanted to accompany him, Flossie got in the way. She was sent to the vet, and I wept for hours over her.

It wasn't that Mother was actively unkind, for she thought far too much of the impression she wanted to make to give one of unkindness. It was just that she didn't care; she was more and more away from home. She visited friends in Dublin and Galway, Birr and Athlone; I never met a woman with so many friends or one so fond of them. All we saw of her was the flurry between one foray and the next as she packed and unpacked. Dad was absorbed in his work, but that was different. He never gave you the same impression of invulnerability as Mother. He came in while she packed, looking like an overgrown schoolboy, in spite of his moustache, and stood with his hands in his trouser pockets and his long neck out, making jokes at her in a mock-vulgar accent. Then, when she grew serious, he put on a blank face and shrugged his shoulders while his thin voice grew squeaky with anxiety – a bit of a nonentity, really, as you could see from the way she took him.

But I who loved her realized that she expected me to be a nonentity, too. She thought Dad made too many demands on her, which you could understand, but she thought the same of me, and sometimes I thought this was also how she must have felt about poor old Flossie.

Things came to a head when she told me she couldn't be at home for my twelfth birthday. There was no particular reason why I should have gone off the handle about that more than about anything else, but I did. The trouble was that the moment I did so, I seemed to have no reasons on my side. I could only sob and stamp and say she hadn't done it to Martha. She looked at me coldly and said I was a pretty picture, that I had no manliness.

'And you did the same to Flossie!' I shouted, stung to madness by her taunt.

I thought she'd hit me, but she only drew herself up, looking twice as noble and beautiful, and her lip curled. 'That is a contemptible remark, Denis,' she said, 'and one I'd expect only from you.'

Then she went off for the evening with the Clarkes, leaving Martha and me alone. Father was still at the office. Martha looked at me half in pity, half in amusement. She was never really very disappointed in Mother, because she expected less of her.

'What did I tell you?' she said.

I went up to my room and cried like a kid. It was the taunt about my lack of manliness that stung me most. I simply felt I couldn't live in the same house any longer with a woman who had said such a thing. I took out my Post Office savings book. I had four pounds fifteen – enough to keep me for a month or more till I found some corner where people wanted me, a plain, rough-spoken chap who only needed a little affection. If the worst came to the worst I could always make for Dublin, where Auntie May and my father's father lived. I knew they'd be glad to help me, because they had never even pretended to like Mother, and though I had resented this in them, I now saw they might have been right. It would be something just to reach their door and say to Auntie May in my plain, straightforward way, 'I see now I was wrong.' Then I dried my eyes, went downstairs, and took out my bicycle. It was equipped with dynamo lamp and everything – a smasher!

'Where are you off to?' Martha asked.

'You'll soon see,' I said darkly, and cycled off.

Then I had my first shock, because as I cycled into Main Street I saw that all the shops were shuttered for the weekly half-day and knew that the post office, too, would be closed. Apart from what I had in the bank I had nothing, and I knew I couldn't get far without money – certainly not as far as I hoped to get, for I intended not to come back.

I stood for ten minutes outside the post office, wondering wildly if one of the clerks would turn up. I felt that I simply couldn't return home. And then the idea struck me that the city was only twenty miles away, and that the post office there was bound to be open. I had been to the city a couple of times with Mother, so there was nothing very unfamiliar or frightening in the idea of it. When I got my money I could either stay the night at a hotel or cycle on through the dark. I was attracted by the latter idea. It would be good fun to cycle through the sleeping villages and towns, and see the dawn break over Dublin, and arrive at Auntie May's door, in the Shelbourne Road, while she was lighting the fire. I could imagine how she would greet me – 'Child of Grace, where did you come from?' 'Ah, just cycled,' I would reply, without any fuss.

It was very pleasant, but it wasn't enough. I cycled slowly and undecidedly out the familiar main road where we walked on Sunday, past the seminary and the little suburban houses. I was still uncertain that I should go on. Then something happened. Suddenly the countryside struck me as strange. I got off my bicycle and looked round. The town had sunk back into its black, bushy hills, with little showing of it but the spire of the church and the ruined tower of the abbey. It was as though it had accompanied me so far and then silently left me and returned. I found myself in new country, with a little, painted town sprawled across a river and, beyond it, bigger, smoother, greener hills. It was a curious sensation, rather like the moment when you find yourself out of your depth and two inclinations struggle in you – one to turn back in panic to the shallows, the other to strike out boldly for the other side.

The mere analogy was enough for me. It was like a challenge, and that moment of panic gave new energy to my cycling. The little town, the big red-brick mansion at the end of a beech avenue, the hexagonal brown building on top of the smooth hill before me, and the glimpses I caught of the river were both fascinating and frightening. I was aware of great distances, of big cloud masses on the horizon, of the fragility of my tyres compared with the rough surface of the road, and everything disappeared in the urgent need to get to the city, to draw out my money, to find myself food and a bed for the night.

For the last ten miles I hadn't even the temptation to look at my surroundings. Things just happened to me: the road bent away under me; wide green rivers rose up and slipped away again under my tyres; castles soared from the roadside with great arches blocked out in masses of shadow. I was lightheaded with hunger. I had been cycling with such savagery that I had exhausted myself, and the spires of the city sticking up from the fields ahead merely presented a fresh problem – whether or not the post office would be open.

Though that is not altogether true. There was one blessed brief spell when the rocky fields closed behind me like a book, and the electric-light poles escorted me up the last hill and gently down between comfortable villas and long gardens to the bridge. The city was stretched out along the other side of the river – a castle by the bridge, a cathedral tower above it, a row of warehouses, a terrace of crumbling Georgian houses – and I felt my heart rise at the thought that whatever happened I had proved I was a man.

But now emerged the greater problem of remaining one. Beyond the bridge the road climbed to the main street, two long façades of red-brick houses broken by the limestone front of a church. As I passed, I promised God to come in and thank Him if the post office was open. But as I crossed its threshold I knew my luck was out. Only the stamp counter was open, everything else was shut. At the stamp counter they told me I must come back next morning. They might as well have told me to come back next year.

Stunned and miserable, I pushed my bike back up to the main street and looked up and down. It was long and wide and lonesome, and I didn't know a soul I could turn to. I knew that without a meal and a rest I couldn't set out for Dublin. I was whacked. I had proved to myself that I was manly, but what good was manliness when Irish post offices wouldn't remain open after five o'clock?

It was just because I was so tired that I went to sit in the church – not out of any confidence in God, who was very much in my black books. I sat in the last row, at the end of the church. It was quiet and dark, with a red light showing far away in the sanctuary. And it was then that the thought of Dad came to me. It was funny that I hadn't thought of him before, even when thinking of Grandfather and Auntie May. I had thought of them as allies in my campaign against Mother. Dad seemed so ineffectual that I hadn't thought of him at all. Now, as I began to imagine him, with his long neck and weak face, his bowler hat and his moustache, which made you think of a fellow dressed up in a school show, his puerile jokes in his vulgar accent, everything about him seemed attractive. And I swear it wasn't only the hunger and panic. It was something new for me; it was almost love. Full of new energy, I knelt and prayed, 'Almighty God, grant I can talk to Dad on the phone!' The sanctuary lamp twinkled conspiratorially, like a signal, and I felt encouraged.

It wasn't as easy as that, though. The first place I asked permission to telephone they just hooshed me out, and the feeling that I was obeying an injunction of Heaven gave place to indignation. The sanctuary lamp had no business making signals unless it could arrange things better. I dawdled hopelessly along the main street, leaving my bike by the kerb and gazing in shop windows. In one I found a mirror where I could see myself full-length. I looked old and heartbroken. It was like a picture. The title 'Homeless' suggested itself to me and I blinked away my tears. There were nice model trains in the window, though – electric ones.

Then, as I passed a public-house, I saw a tall man in shirtsleeves by the door. I had a feeling that he had been watching me for a good while. He winked, and I winked back.

'Is it a pint you're looking for?' he asked in a loud, jovial tone, and I was disappointed, because it struck me that he might be only looking for trade.

'No,' I said, though I shouldn't have said it if he had asked me whether I was looking for lemonade.

'I'm sorry,' he said. 'I thought you might be a customer. Are you from these parts?'

'No,' I said modestly, conscious that I had travelled a long distance, but not wishing to boast, 'I'm from Boharna.'

'Boharna, begod!' he exclaimed, with new interest. 'And what are you doing in town?'

'I ran away from home,' I said, feeling I might as well get that in, in case he could help me.

'You couldn't do better,' he said with enthusiasm. 'I did it myself.'

'Did you?' I asked eagerly. This seemed the very sort of man I wanted to meet. 'When was this?'

'When I was fourteen.'

'I'm only twelve,' I said.

'There's nothing like beginning young,' he said. 'I did it three times in all before I got away with it. They were fed up with me then. You have to keep plugging away at it. Is it your old fellow?'

'No,' I said, surrendering myself to his experience and even adopting his broad way of speech. 'My old one.'

'Ah, cripes, that's tough,' he said. ' 'Tis bad enough having the old man on your back, but 'tis the devil entirely when you haven't the old woman behind you. And where are you off to now?'

'I don't know,' I admitted. 'I wanted to go to Dublin, but I can't.'

'Why not?'

'All my money is in the savings bank and I can't get it till tomorrow.'

'That's bad management, you know,' he said, shaking his head. 'You should have it with you.'

'I know,' I said, 'but I only made up my mind today.'

'Ah, cripes,' he said, 'you should have a thing like that planned for months ahead. 'Tis easy seen you're not used to it. It looks as if you might have to go back.'

'I can't go back,' I said despondently. ' 'Tis twenty miles. If I could only talk to Dad on the phone, he'd tell me what to do.'

'Who is your dad?' he asked, and I told him. 'Ah, we might be able to manage that for you. Come in.'

There was a phone in the corner, and he beckoned me to fire ahead. After a few minutes I heard Dad's voice, faint and squeaky with surprise, and I almost wept with delight.

'Hullo, son,' he said. 'Where on earth are you?'

'In Asragh, Daddy,' I said lightly. Even then I couldn't make a lot of it, the way another fellow would.

'Asragh?' Dad said, and I could almost see how his eyebrows worked up his forehead. 'What took you there?'

'I just ran away from home, Dad,' I said, trying to make it sound casual.

'Oh!' he said, and he paused for a moment, but his voice didn't change either. 'How did you get there?'

'On the bike, Dad.'

'The whole way?'

'The whole way.'

'Are you dead?' he asked with a laugh.

'Ah, just a bit,' I said modestly.

'Have you had anything to eat?'

'No, Dad.'

'Why not? Didn't you bring any money with you?'

'Only my savings-bank book, but the post office is shut.'

'Oh, hard luck!' he said. 'And what are you going to do now?'

'I don't know, Dad. I thought you might tell me.'

'Well, what about coming home?'

'I don't mind, Dad. Whatever you say.'

'Hold on a minute now till I see when the next bus is . . . Oh, hullo! You can get one in forty minutes' time – seven-ten. Tell the conductor I'll meet you and pay your fare. Is that all right?'

'That's grand, Dad,' I said, feeling that the world had almost come right again.

'Good! I'll have some supper ready. Mind yourself now.'

When I finished, the barman was waiting for me with his coat on. He had a girl looking after the bar for him.

'Better come and have a cup of tea with me before the bus,' he said. 'We can leave the old bike here.'

The lights were just being switched on. We sat in a brilliantly lit café, and I ate cake after cake and drank hot tea while the barman told me how he had run away. You could see he was a real reckless sort. On the first two occasions he had been caught by the police. The first time he had pinched a bicycle and cycled all the way to Dublin, sleeping in barns and deserted cottages. The third time he had joined the Army and not come home for years. It seemed that running away was not so easy as I had thought. On the other hand, it was much more adventurous. I felt the least shade sorry that I hadn't planned more carefully, and resolved to have everything ready if I did it again.

He put me and my bicycle on the bus and insisted on paying my fare. He also made me promise to tell Dad that he had paid my fare and that Dad owed me the money. He said in this world you had to stick up for your rights. He was a rough chap, but you could see he had a heart of gold. It struck me that only rough chaps like us were really that way and I promised to send him a letter.

When the bus drew up before the hotel, Dad was there,

with his bowler hat, and with his long neck anxiously craned to find me.

'Well, the gouger!' he chuckled in his commonest accent. 'Who'd think the son of a decent, good-living man like me would turn into a common pedestrian tramp? Did you get an old bone in the doss-house, mate?'

I felt it was only right to keep my promise to the barman, so I told him about the fare, and he laughed like a kid and gave me the money. Then, as he pushed my bike down the main street, I asked the question that had been on my mind since I had heard his voice on the phone. 'Mummy back yet, Dad?' What I really meant, of course, was 'Does she know?' But I couldn't put it like that – not to him.

His face changed at once. It became strained and serious again. 'No, son, not yet,' he said. 'Probably won't be in before ten or eleven.'

I was torn with the desire to ask him not to mention it to her, but it choked me. It would have seemed too much like the very thing I had always blamed Martha for – ganging up against Mother. At the same time I thought that maybe he was thinking the same thing, because he mentioned with careful casualness that he had sent Martha to the pictures. We had supper when we got home, and when we washed up together afterwards, I knew I was right.

Mother came in, and he talked as though nothing had happened, questioned her about her day, shrugged his shoulders over his own, looked blank and nervous. He had never seemed more a nonentity than then, but for the first time I realized how superficial that impression was. It was curious, watching him create understanding between us, understanding in more ways than one, for I realized that, like myself and the barman, Dad, too, had run away from home at some time in the past, and for some reason – perhaps because the bank was shut or because he was hungry, tired, and lonely – he had come back. People mostly came back, but their protest remained to distinguish them from all the others who had never run away. It was the real sign of their manhood.

I never ran away again after that. There was no need for it, because the strands that had bound me so inescapably to my mother seemed to have parted.

A MINORITY

DENIS HALLIGAN noticed Willy Stein for the first time one Sunday when the other fellows were at Mass. As Denis was a Protestant, he didn't go to Mass. Instead, he sat on the steps outside the chapel with Willy. Willy was a thin, seedy little chap with long, wild hair. It was an autumn morning; there was mist on the trees, and you could scarcely see the great ring of mountains that cut them off there in the middle of Ireland, miles from anywhere.

'Why did they send you here if you're a Proddy?' asked Willy.

'I don't know,' said Denis, who felt his background was so queer that he didn't want to explain it to anybody. 'I suppose because it was cheap.'

'Is your old fellow a Catholic?' asked Willy.

'No,' replied Denis. 'Is yours?'

'No,' Willy said contemptuously. 'He was a Proddy. My old one was a Proddy, too.'

'Where do they live?' asked Denis.

'They're dead,' Willy said, making the motion of spitting. 'The bloody Germans killed them.'

'Oh, cripes!' Denis said regretfully. Denis had a great admiration for everything German, particularly tank generals, and when he grew up he wanted to be a tank general himself, but it seemed a pity that they had to kill Willy's father and mother. Bad as it was to have your parents separated, as his own were, it was worse having them dead. 'Was it a bomb?' he asked.

'No,' Willy replied without undue emotion. 'They were killed in a camp. They sent me over to the Cumminses in Dublin or I'd have been killed, too. The Cumminses are Catholics. That's why I was sent here.'

'Do you like it here?' asked Denis.

'I do not,' Willy said scornfully in his slummy Dublin accent, and then took out a slingshot and fitted a stone in it. 'I'd sooner Vienna. Vienna was gas. When I grow up I'm going to get out of this blooming place.'

'But what will you do?'

'Aw, go to sea, or something. I don't care.'

Denis was interested in Willy. Apart from the fact that they were the only Proddies in the school, Willy struck him as being really tough, and Denis admired toughness. He was always trying to be tough himself, but there was a soft streak in him that kept breaking out. It was breaking out now, and he knew it. Though he saw that Willy didn't give a rap about his parents, Denis couldn't help being sorry for him, alone in the middle of Ireland with his father and mother dead half a world away. He said as much to his friend Nigel Healy, from Cork, that afternoon, but Nigel only gave a superior sniff.

'But that fellow is mad,' he said, in his reasonable way.

'How is he mad?' asked Denis.

'He's not even left go home on holidays,' explained Nigel. 'He has to stay here all during the summer. Those people were nice to him, and what does he do? Breaks every window in the place. They had the police to the house twice. He's mad on slingshots.'

'He had one this morning,' said Denis.

'Last time he was caught with one he got flogged,' said Nigel. 'You see, the fellow has no sense. I even saw him putting sugar on his meat.'

'But why did he do that?' asked Denis.

'Said he liked it,' replied Nigel with a smile and a shrug.

'He's bound to get expelled one of these days. You'd want to mind yourself with him.'

But for some reason that only made Denis more interested in Willy Stein, and he looked forward to meeting him again by himself the following Sunday. He was curious to know why the Germans would want to kill Stein's father and mother. That seemed to him a funny thing to do – unless, of course, they were spies for the English.

Again they sat on the steps, but this morning the sun was warm and bright, and the mountains all round them were a brilliant blue. If Stein's parents were really spies, the idea of it did not seem to have occurred to him. According to him, his father had been a lawyer and his mother something on a newspaper, and he didn't seem to remember much about them except that they were both 'gas'. Everything with Stein was 'gas'. His mother was gentle and timid, and let him have everything he wanted, so she was 'great gas'. His father was sure she was ruining him, and was always on to him to study and be better than other kids, and when his father got like that he used to weep and shout and wave his hands, but that was only now and then. He was gas, too, though not, Denis gathered, great gas. Willy suddenly waved his hands and shouted something in a foreign language.

'What's that?' asked Denis with the deepest admiration.

'German,' Stein replied, in his graceless way.

'What does it mean?' asked Denis.

'I dunno,' Stein said lightly.

Denis was disappointed. For a fellow like himself, who was interested in tanks, a spatter of German might one day be useful. He had the impression that Stein was only letting on to remember parents he had lost before he was really old enough to remember them.

Their talk was interrupted by Father Houlihan, a tall, morose-looking priest. He had a bad belly and a worse temper, but Denis knew Father Houlihan liked him, and he admired Father Houlihan. He was violent, but he wasn't a stinker.

'Hah!' he said, in his mocking way. 'And what do you two cock sparrows think you're doing out here?'

'We're excused, Father,' Denis said brightly, leaping to his feet.

'No one is excused anything in this place till I excuse him,' snarled Father Houlihan cheerfully, 'and I don't excuse much. Run into Mass now, ye pair of heathens!'

'But we're Protestants, Father!' Stein cried, and Denis was half afraid of seeing the red flush on Father Houlihan's forehead that showed he was out for blood.

'Aha, what fine Protestants we have in ye!' he snorted good-humouredly. 'I suppose you have a Protestant slingshot in your pocket at this very minute, you scoundrel, you!'

'I have not!' Stein shouted. 'You know Murphy took it off me.'

'Mr Murphy to you, Willy Stein,' said the priest, pinching his ear playfully and pushing him towards the chapel. 'And next time I catch you with a slingshot I'll give you a Catholic cane on your fat Protestant backside.'

The two boys went into chapel and sat together on a bench at the back. Willy was muttering indignantly to himself, but he waited until everyone was kneeling with bowed head. Then, to Denis' horror, he took out a slingshot and a bit of paper, which he chewed up into a wet ball. There was nothing hasty or spontaneous about this. Stein went about it with a concentration that was almost pious. As the bell rang for the Consecration, there was a *ping*, and a seminarist kneeling at the side of the chapel put his hand to his ear and looked angrily round. But by this time Stein had thrown himself on his knees, and his eyes were shut in a look of rapt devotion. It gave Denis quite a turn. Even if he wasn't a Catholic, he had been brought up to respect every form of religion.

The business of going to Mass and feeling out of it made

Denis Halligan completely fed up with being a Proddy. He had never liked it anyway, even at home, as a kid. He was gregarious, and a born gang leader, a promoter of organization, and it cut him to the heart to feel that at any moment he might be deserted by his gang because, through no fault of his own, he was not a Catholic and might accidentally say or do the wrong thing. He even resented the quiet persuasion that the school authorities exercised on him. A senior called Hanley, whom Nigel described sarcastically as 'Halligan's angel', was attached to Denis – not to proselytize, but to give him an intelligent understanding of the religious life of the group. Hanley had previously been attached to Stein, but that had proved hopeless, because Stein seemed to take Hanley's company as a guarantee of immunity from punishment, so he merely involved Hanley in every form of forbidden activity, from smoking to stealing. One day when Stein stole a gold tie-pin from a master's room, Hanley had to report him. On Hanley's account, he was not flogged, but told to put the tie-pin back in the place from which he had taken it. Stein did so, and seized the opportunity to pinch five shillings instead, and this theft was discovered only when someone saw Stein fast asleep in bed with his mouth open and the two half-crowns in his jaw. As Hanley, a sweet and saintly boy, said to Denis, it wasn't Stein's fault. He was just unbalanced.

In any other circumstances Denis would have enjoyed Hanley's attention, but it made him mad to be singled out like this and looked after like some kid who couldn't undo his own buttons.

'Listen, Hanley,' he said angrily one day when he and Nigel were discussing football and Hanley had slipped a little homily into the conversation. 'It's no good preaching at me. It's not my fault that I'm a Proddy.'

'Well, you don't have to be a Proddy if you don't want to be,' Hanley said with a smile. 'Do you?'

'How can I help it?' asked Denis.

'Well, who'd stop you?'

'My mother would, for one.'

'Did you try?'

'What do you mean, Hanley?'

'I mean, why don't you ask her?' Hanley went on, in the same bland way. 'I wouldn't be too sure she wants you to be a Proddy.'

'How could I ask her?'

'You could write. Or phone,' Hanley added hastily, seeing the look on Denis' face at the notion of writing an extra letter. 'Father Houlihan would let you use the telephone, if you asked him. Or I'll ask him, if you like.'

'Do if you want to,' said Denis. 'I don't care.'

He didn't really believe his mother would agree to something he wanted, just like that, but he had no objection to a free telephone call that would enable him to hear her voice again. To his astonishment, she made no difficulty about it.

'Why, of course, darling,' she said sweetly. 'If that's how you feel and Father Houlihan has no objection, I don't mind. You know I only want you to be happy at school.'

It was a colossal relief. Overnight, his whole position in the school changed. He had ceased to be an outsider. He was one of the gang. He might even be Chief Gang Leader in the course of time. He was a warm-hearted boy, and he had the feeling that by a simple gesture he had conferred an immense benefit on everybody. The only person who didn't seem too enthusiastic was Father Houlihan, but then he was not much of an enthusiast anyway. 'My bold young convert,' he said, pulling Denis' ear, 'I suppose any day now you'll start paying attention to your lessons.'

Yet the moment he had made his decision, he began to feel guilty about young Stein. As has been said, he was not only gregarious, but he was also a born gang leader, and had the feeling that someone might think he had deserted an ally to secure his own advantage. He was suddenly filled with a wild desire to convert Willy as well, so that the pair of them could be received as a group. He saw it as even more of a duty of Willy's than of his own. Willy had been saved from his parents' fate by a good kind Catholic family, and it was the least they could expect that Willy should show his gratitude to them, to the school, and to Ireland.

But Willy seemed to have a deplorable head for theology. All the time they talked Denis had the impression that Willy was only planning some fresh mischief.

'Ah, come on, Willy,' he said authoritatively, 'you don't want to be a blooming old Proddy.'

'I don't want to be a Cat either,' said Willy with a shrug.

'Don't you want to be like the other fellows in the school?'

'Why don't they want to be like me?' asked Stein.

'Because there's only two of us, and there's hundreds of them. And they're right.'

'And if there were hundreds of us and two of them, we'd be right, I suppose?' Stein said with a sneer. 'You want to be like the rest of them. All right, be like the rest of them, but let me alone.'

'I'm only speaking for your own good,' Denis said, getting mad. What really made him mad was the feeling that somehow Stein wasn't speaking to him at all; that inside, he was as lonely and lost as Denis would have been in similar circumstances, and he wouldn't admit to it, wouldn't break down as Denis would have done. What he really wanted to do was to give Stein a sock in the gob, but he knew that even this was no good. Stein was always being beaten, and he always yelled bloody murder, and next day he came back and did the same thing again. Everyone was thinking exclusively of Stein's good, and it always ended up by their beating him, and it never did him any good at all.

Denis confided his difficulties to Hanley, who was also full of concern for Stein's good, but Hanley only smiled sadly and shook his head.

'I know more about that than you do, Denis,' he said, in his fatherly way. 'I'll tell you if you promise not to repeat it to a living soul.'

'What is it?' asked Denis eagerly.

'Promise! Mind, this is serious!'

'Oh, I promise.'

'The fact is that Stein isn't a Proddy at all,' Hanley said sadly.

'But what is he?'

'Stein is a Jew,' Hanley said in a low voice. 'That's why his father and mother were killed. Nobody knows that, though.'

'But does Stein know he's a Jew?' Denis asked excitedly.

'No. And mind, we're not supposed to know it, either. Nobody knows it, except the priests and ourselves.'

'But why doesn't somebody tell him?'

'Because if they did, he might blab about it – you know, he's not very smart – and then all the fellows would be jeering at him. Remember, Denis, if you ever mentioned it, Father Houlihan would skin you alive. He says Stein is after suffering enough. He's sorry for Stein. Mind, I'm only warning you.'

'But won't it be awful for him when he finds out?'

'When he's older and has a job, he won't mind it so much,' said Hanley.

But Denis wasn't sure. Somehow, he had an idea that Stein wanted to stay a Proddy simply because that was what his father and mother had been and it was now the only link he had with them, and if someone would just tell him, he wouldn't care so much and would probably become a Catholic, like Denis. Afterwards, when he did find out that everything he had done was mistaken, it might be too late. And this – and the fact that Father Houlihan, whom Denis admired, was also sorry for Willy Stein – increased his feeling of guilt, and he almost wished he hadn't been in such a hurry himself about being converted. Denis wasn't a bright student, but he was a born officer and he would never have deserted his men.

The excitement of his own reception into the Church almost banished the thought of Stein from his mind. On the Sunday he was received he was allowed to sleep late, and Murphy, the seminarist, even brought him comics to read in bed. This was real style! Then he dressed in his best suit and went down to meet his mother, who arrived, with his sister, Martha, in a hired car. For once, Martha was deferential. She was impressed, and the sight of the chapel impressed her even more. In front of the High Altar there was an isolated prie-dieu for Denis himself, and behind him a special pew was reserved for her and his mother.

Denis knew afterwards that he hadn't made a single false move. Only once was his exaltation disturbed, and that was when he heard the *ping* of a slingshot and realized that Stein, sitting by himself in the back row, was whiling away the time by getting into fresh mischief. The rage rose up in Denis, in spite of all his holy thoughts, and for a moment he resolved that when it was all over he would find Willy Stein and beat him to a jelly.

Instead, when it was over he suddenly felt weary. Martha had ceased to be impressed by him. Now she was just a sister a bare year younger who was mad with him for having stolen the attention of everybody. She knew only too well what a figure she would have cut as a convert, and was crazy with jealousy.

'I won't stand it,' she said. 'I'm going to be a Catholic, too.'

'Well, who's stopping you?' Denis asked.

'Nobody's going to stop me,' said Martha. 'Just because Daddy is fond of you doesn't mean that I can't be a Catholic.'

'What has Daddy to do with it?' asked Denis with a feeling of alarm.

'Because now that you're a Catholic, the courts wouldn't let him have you,' Martha said excitedly. 'Because Daddy is an atheist, or something, and he wanted to get hold of you. He tried to get you away from Mummy. I don't care about Daddy. I'm going to be converted, too.'

'Go on!' growled Denis, feeling sadly how his mood of exaltation was fading. 'You're only an old copycat.'

'I am not a copycat, Denis Halligan,' she said bitterly. 'It's only that you always sucked up to Daddy and I didn't, and he doesn't care about me. I don't care about him, either, so there!'

Denis felt a sudden pang of terror at her words. In a dim sort of way he realized that what he had done might have consequences he had never contemplated. He had no wish to live with his father, but his father came to the school to see him sometimes, and he had always had the feeling that if he ever got fed up with living at home with his mother and Martha, his father would always have him. Nobody had told him that by becoming a Catholic he had made it impossible for his father to have him. He glanced round and saw Stein, thin and pale and furtive, slouching away from the chapel with his hand in his pocket clutching his slingshot. He gave Denis a grin in which there was no malice, but Denis scowled and looked away.

'Who's that?' asked Martha inquisitively.

'Oh, him!' Denis said contemptuously. 'That's only a dirty Jew-boy.'

Yet even as he spoke the words he knew they were false. What he really felt towards Willy Stein was an aching envy. Nobody had told him that by changing his faith he might be unfaithful to his father, but nobody had told Stein, either, and, alone and despairing, he still clung to a faith that was not his own for the sake of a father and mother he had already almost forgotten, who had been murdered half a world away and whom he would never see again. For a single moment Denis saw the dirty little delinquent whom everyone pitied and despised transfigured by a glory that he himself would never know.

(1957)

THE FACE OF EVIL

I could never understand all the old talk about how hard it is to be a saint. I was a saint for quite a bit of my life and I never saw anything hard in it. And when I stopped being a saint, it wasn't because the life was too hard.

I fancy it is the sissies who make it seem like that. We had quite a few of them in school, fellows whose mothers intended them to be saints, and who hadn't the nerve to be anything else. I never enjoyed the society of chaps who wouldn't commit sin for the same reason that they wouldn't dirty their new suits. That was never what sanctity meant to me, and I doubt if it is what it means to other saints. The companions I liked were the tough gang down the road, and I enjoyed going down of an evening and talking with them under the gaslamp about football matches and school, even if they did sometimes say things I wouldn't say myself. I was never one for criticizing; I had enough to do criticizing myself, and I knew they were decent chaps and didn't really mean much harm by the things they said about girls.

No, for me the main attraction of being a saint was the way it always gave you something to do. You could never say you felt time hanging on your hands. It was like having a room of your own to keep tidy; you'd scour it, and put everything neatly back in its place, and within an hour or two it was beginning to look as untidy as ever. It was a full-time job that began when you woke and stopped only when you fell asleep.

I would wake in the morning, for instance, and think how

nice it was to lie in bed, and congratulate myself on not
having to get up for another half-hour. That was enough.
Instantly a sort of alarm clock would go off in my mind; the
mere thought that I could enjoy half an hour's comfort
would make me aware of an alternative, and I'd begin an
argument with myself. I had a voice in me that was almost
the voice of a stranger, the way it nagged and jeered. Sometimes I could almost visualize it, and then it took on the
appearance of a fat and sneering teacher I had some years
before at school – a man I really hated. I hated that voice. It
always began in the same way, smooth and calm and
dangerous. I could see the teacher rubbing his fat hands and
smirking.

'Don't get alarmed, boy. You're in no hurry. You have
another half-hour.'

'I know well I have another half-hour,' I would reply,
trying to keep my temper. 'What harm am I doing? I'm only
imagining I'm down in a submarine. Is there anything
wrong in that?'

'Oho, not the least in the world. I'd say there's been a
heavy frost. Just the sort of morning when there's ice in the
bucket.'

'And what has that to do with it?'

'Nothing, I tell you. Of course, for people like you it's easy
enough in the summer months, but the least touch of frost in
the air soon makes you feel different. I wouldn't worry
trying to keep it up. You haven't the stuff for this sort of life
at all.'

And gradually my own voice grew weaker as that of my
tormentor grew stronger, till all at once I would strip the
clothes from off myself and lie in my nightshirt, shivering
and muttering, 'So I haven't the stuff in me, haven't I?' Then
I would go downstairs before my parents were awake, strip
and wash in the bucket, ice or no ice, and when Mother
came down she would cry in alarm, 'Child of Grace, what
has you up at this hour? Sure, 'tis only half past seven.' She

almost took it as a reproach to herself, poor woman, and I couldn't tell her the reason, and even if I could have done so, I wouldn't. How could you say to anybody 'I want to be a saint'?

Then I went to Mass and enjoyed again the mystery of the streets and lanes in the early morning; the frost which made your feet clatter off the walls at either side of you like falling masonry, and the different look that everything wore, as though, like yourself, it was all cold and scrubbed and new. In the winter the lights would still be burning red in the little cottages, and in summer they were ablaze with sunshine so that their interiors were dimmed to shadows. Then there were the different people, all of whom recognized one another, like Mrs MacEntee, who used to be a stewardess on the boats, and Macken, the tall postman, people who seemed ordinary enough when you met them during the day, but carried something of their mystery with them at Mass, as though they, too, were reborn.

I can't pretend I was ever very good at school, but even there it was a help. I might not be clever, but I had always a secret reserve of strength to call on in the fact that I had what I wanted, and that beside it I wanted nothing. People frequently gave me things, like fountain pens or pencil-sharpeners, and I would suddenly find myself becoming attached to them and immediately know I must give them away, and then feel the richer for it. Even without throwing my weight around I could help and protect kids younger than myself, and yet not become involved in their quarrels. Not to become involved, to remain detached – that was the great thing; to care for things and for people, yet not to care for them so much that your happiness became dependent on them.

It was like no other hobby, because you never really got the better of yourself, and all at once you would suddenly find yourself reverting to childish attitudes; flaring up in a wax with some fellow, or sulking when Mother asked you

to go for a message, and then it all came back; the nagging
of the infernal alarm clock which grew louder with every
moment until it incarnated as a smooth, fat, jeering face.

'Now, that's the first time you've behaved sensibly for
months, boy. That was the right way to behave to your
mother.'

'Well, it *was* the right way. Why can't she let me alone,
once in a while? I only want to read. I suppose I'm entitled
to a bit of peace some time?'

'Ah, of course you are, my dear fellow. Isn't that what I'm
saying? Go on with your book! Imagine you're a cowboy,
riding to the rescue of a beautiful girl in a cabin in the woods,
and let that silly woman go for the messages herself. She
probably hasn't long to live anyway, and when she dies
you'll be able to do all the weeping you like.'

And suddenly tears of exasperation would come to my
eyes and I'd heave the story book to the other side of the
room and shout back at the voice that gave me no rest,
'Cripes, I might as well be dead and buried. I have no blooming life.' After that I would apologize to Mother (who, poor
woman, was more embarrassed than anything else and as-
sured me that it was all her fault), go on the message, and
write another tick in my notebook against the heading of
'Bad Temper' so as to be able to confess it to Father O'Regan
when I went to Confession on Saturday. Not that he was
ever severe with me, no matter what I did; he thought I was
the last word in holiness, and was always asking me to pray
for some special intention of his own. And though I was
depressed, I never lost interest, for no matter what I did I
could scarcely ever reduce the total of times I had to
tick off that item in my notebook.

Oh, I don't pretend it was any joke, but it did give you the
feeling that your life had some meaning; that inside you, you
had a real source of strength; that there was nothing you
could not do without, and yet remain sweet, self-sufficient,
and content. Sometimes too, there was the feeling of some-

thing more than mere content, as though your body were transparent, like a window, and light shone through it as well as on it, onto the road, the houses, and the playing children, as though it were you who was shining on them, and tears of happiness would come into my eyes, and I would hurl myself among the playing children just to forget it.

But, as I say, I had no inclination to mix with other kids who might be saints as well. The fellow who really fascinated me was a policeman's son named Dalton, who was easily the most vicious kid in the locality. The Daltons lived on the terrace above ours. Mrs Dalton was dead; there was a younger brother called Stevie, who was next door to an imbecile, and there was something about that kid's cheerful grin that was even more frightening than the malice on Charlie's broad face. Their father was a tall, melancholy man, with a big black moustache, and the nearest thing imaginable to one of the Keystone cops. Everyone was sorry for his loss in his wife, but you knew that if it hadn't been that it would have been something else – maybe the fact that he hadn't lost her. Charlie was only an additional grief. He was always getting into trouble, stealing and running away from home; and only his father's being a policeman prevented his being sent to an industrial school. One of my most vivid recollections is that of Charlie's education. I'd hear a shriek, and there would be Mr Dalton, dragging Charlie along the pavement to school, and whenever the names his son called him grew a little more obscene than usual, pausing to give Charlie a good going-over with the belt which he carried loose in his hand. It is an exceptional father who can do this without getting some pleasure out of it, but Mr Dalton looked as though even that were an additional burden. Charlie's screams could always fetch me out.

'What is it?' Mother would cry after me.

'Ah, nothing. Only Charlie Dalton again.'

'Come in! Come in!'

'I won't be seen.'

'Come in, I say. 'Tis never right.'

And even when Charlie uttered the most atrocious indecencies, she only joined her hands as if in prayer and muttered, 'The poor child! The poor unfortunate child!' I never could understand the way she felt about Charlie. He wouldn't have been Charlie if it hadn't been for the leatherings and the threats of the industrial school.

Looking back on it, the funniest thing is that I seemed to be the only fellow on the road he didn't hate. The rest were all terrified of him, and some of the kids would go a mile to avoid him. He was completely unclassed: being a policeman's son, he should have been way up the social scale, but he hated the respectable kids worse than the others. When we stood under the gaslamp at night and saw him coming up the road, everybody fell silent. He looked suspiciously at the group, ready to spring at anyone's throat if he saw the shadow of offence; ready even when there wasn't a shadow. He fought like an animal, by instinct, without judgement, and without ever reckoning the odds, and he was terribly strong. He wasn't clever; several of the older chaps could beat him to a frazzle when it was merely a question of boxing or wrestling, but it never was that with Dalton. He was out for blood and usually got it. Yet he was never that way with me. We weren't friends. All that ever happened when we passed one another was that I smiled at him and got a cold, cagey nod in return. Sometimes we stopped and exchanged a few words, but it was an ordeal because we never had anything to say to one another.

It was like the signalling of ships, or more accurately, the courtesies of great powers. I tried, like Mother, to be sorry for him in having no proper home, and getting all those leatherings, but the feeling which came uppermost in me was never pity but respect: respect for a fellow who had done all the things I would never do: stolen money, stolen

bicycles, run away from home, slept with tramps and crimi-
nals in barns and doss-houses, and ridden without a ticket on
trains and on buses. It filled my imagination. I have a vivid
recollection of one summer morning when I was going up
the hill to Mass. Just as I reached the top and saw the low,
sandstone church perched high up ahead of me, he poked his
bare head round the corner of a lane to see who was coming.
It startled me. He was standing with his back to the gable of
a house; his face was dirty and strained; it was broad and
lined, and the eyes were very small, furtive and flickering,
and sometimes a sort of spasm would come over them and
they flickered madly for half a minute on end.

'Hullo, Charlie,' I said. 'Where were you?'

'Out,' he replied shortly.

'All night?' I asked in astonishment.

'Yeh,' he replied with a nod.

'What are you doing now?'

He gave a short, bitter laugh.

'Waiting till my old bastard of a father goes out to work
and I can go home.'

His eyes flickered again, and selfconsciously he drew his
hand across them as though pretending they were tired.

'I'll be late for Mass,' I said uneasily. 'So long.'

'So long.'

That was all, but all the time at Mass, among the flowers
and the candles, watching the beautiful, sad old face of Mrs
MacEntee and the plump, smooth, handsome face of
Macken, the postman, I was haunted by the image of that
other face, wild and furtive and dirty, peering round a
corner like an animal looking from its burrow. When I came
out, the morning was brilliant over the valley below me; the
air was punctuated with bugle calls from the cliff where the
barrack stood, and Charlie Dalton was gone. No, it wasn't
pity I felt for him. It wasn't even respect. It was almost like
envy.

Then, one Saturday evening, an incident occurred which

changed my attitude to him; indeed, changed my attitude to myself, though it wasn't until long after that I realized it. I was on my way to Confession, preparatory to Communion next morning. I always went to Confession at the parish church in town where Father O'Regan was. As I passed the tramway terminus at the Cross, I saw Charlie sitting on the low wall above the Protestant church, furtively smoking the butt-end of a cigarette which somebody had dropped getting on the tram. Another tram arrived as I reached the Cross, and a number of people alighted and went off in different directions. I crossed the road to Charlie and he gave me his most distant nod.

'Hullo.'

'Hullo, Cha. Waiting for somebody?'

'No. Where are you off to?'

'Confession.'

'Huh.' He inhaled the cigarette butt deeply and then tossed it over his shoulder into the sunken road beneath without looking where it alighted. 'You go a lot.'

'Every week,' I said modestly.

'Jesus!' he said with a short laugh. 'I wasn't there for twelve months.'

I shrugged my shoulders. As I say, I never went in much for criticizing others, and, anyway, Charlie wouldn't have been Charlie if he had gone to Confession every week.

'Why do you go so often?' he asked challengingly.

'Oh, I don't know,' I said doubtfully. 'I suppose it keeps you out of harm's way.'

'But you don't do any harm,' he growled, just as though he were defending me against someone who had been attacking me.

'Ah, we all do harm.'

'But, Jesus Christ, you don't do anything,' he said almost angrily, and his eyes flickered again in that curious nervous spasm, and almost as if they put him into a rage, he drove his knuckles into them.

'We all do things,' I said. 'Different things.'

'Well, what do you do?'

'I lose my temper a lot,' I admitted.

'Jesus!' he said again and rolled his eyes.

'It's a sin just the same,' I said obstinately.

'A sin? Losing your temper? Jesus, I want to kill people. I want to kill my bloody old father, for one. I will too, one of those days. Take a knife to him.'

'I know, I know,' I said, at a loss to explain what I meant. 'But that's just the same thing as me.'

I wished to God I could talk better. It wasn't any missionary zeal. I was excited because for the first time I knew that Charlie felt about me exactly as I felt about him, with a sort of envy, and I wanted to explain to him that he didn't have to envy me, and that he could be as much a saint as I was just as I could be as much a sinner as he was. I wanted to explain that it wasn't a matter of tuppence ha'penny worth of sanctity as opposed to tuppence worth that made the difference, that it wasn't what you did, but what you lost by doing it, that mattered. The whole Cross had become a place of mystery; the grey light, drained of warmth; the trees hanging over the old crumbling walls, the tram, shaking like a boat when someone mounted it. It was the way I sometimes felt afterwards with a girl, as though everything about you melted and fused and became one with a central mystery.

'But when what you do isn't any harm?' he repeated angrily, with that flickering of the eyes I had almost come to dread.

'Look, Cha,' I said, 'you can't say a thing isn't any harm. Everything is harm. It might be losing my temper with me and murder with you, like you say, but it would only come to the same thing. If I show you something, will you promise not to tell?'

'Why would I tell?'

'But promise.'

'Oh, all right.'

Then I took out my little notebook and showed it to him. It was extraordinary, and I knew it was extraordinary. I found myself, sitting on that wall, showing a notebook I wouldn't have shown to anyone else in the world to Charlie Dalton, a fellow any kid on the road would go a long way to avoid, and yet I had the feeling that he would understand it as no one else would do. My whole life was there, under different headings – Disobedience, Bad Temper, Bad Thoughts, Selfishness, and Laziness – and he looked through quietly, studying the ticks I had placed against each count.

'You see,' I said, 'you talk about your father, but look at all the things I do against my mother. I know she's a good mother, but if she's sick or if she can't walk fast when I'm in town with her, I get mad just as you do. It doesn't matter what sort of mother or father you have. It's what you do to yourself when you do things like that.'

'What do you do to yourself?' he asked quietly.

'It's hard to explain. It's only a sort of peace you have inside yourself. And you can't be just good, no matter how hard you try. You can only do your best, and if you do your best you feel peaceful inside. It's like when I miss Mass of a morning. Things mightn't be any harder on me that day than any other day, but I'm not as well able to stand up to them. It makes things a bit different for the rest of the day. You don't mind it so much if you get a hammering. You know there's something else in the world besides the hammering.'

I knew it was a feeble description of what morning Mass really meant to me, the feeling of strangeness which lasted throughout the whole day, and reduced reality to its real proportions, but it was the best I could do. I hated leaving him.

'I'll be late for Confession,' I said regretfully, getting off the wall.

'I'll go down a bit of the way with you,' he said, giving a

last glance at my notebook and handing it back to me. I knew he was being tempted to come to Confession along with me, but my pleasure had nothing to do with that. As I say, I never had any missionary zeal. It was the pleasure of understanding rather than that of conversion.

He came down the steps to the church with me and we went in together.

'I'll wait here for you,' he whispered, and sat in one of the back pews.

It was dark there; there were just a couple of small, un-shaded lights in the aisles above the confessionals. There was a crowd of old women outside Father O'Regan's box, so I knew I had a long time to wait. Old women never got done with their confessions. For the first time I felt it long, but when my turn came it was all over in a couple of minutes: the usual 'Bless you, my child. Say a prayer for me, won't you?' When I came out, I saw Charlie Dalton sitting among the old women outside the confessional, waiting to go in. I felt very happy about it in a quiet way, and when I said my penance I said a special prayer for him.

It struck me that he was a long time inside, and I began to grow worried. Then he came out, and I saw by his face that it was no good. It was the expression of someone who is saying to himself with a sort of evil triumph, 'There, I told you what it was like.'

'It's all right,' he whispered, giving his belt a hitch. 'You go home.'

'I'll wait for you,' I said.

'I'll be a good while.'

I knew then Father O'Regan had given him a heavy pen-ance, and my heart sank.

'It doesn't matter,' I said. 'I'll wait.'

And it was only long afterwards that it occurred to me that I might have taken one of the major decisions of my life without being aware of it. I sat at the back of the church in the dusk and waited for him. He was kneeling up in front, before the altar, and I knew it was no good. At first I was too stunned to feel. All I knew was that my happiness had all gone. I admired Father O'Regan; I knew that Charlie must have done things that I couldn't even imagine – terrible things – but the resentment grew in me. What right had Father O'Regan or anyone to treat him like that? Because he was down, people couldn't help wanting to crush him further. For the first time in my life I knew real temptation. I wanted to go with Charlie and share his fate. For the first time I realized that the life before me would have complexities of emotion which I couldn't even imagine.

The following week he ran away from home again, took a bicycle, broke into a shop to steal cigarettes, and, after being arrested seventy-five miles from Cork in a little village on the coast, was sent to an industrial school.

(1954)

THE TEACHER'S MASS

FATHER FOGARTY, the curate in Crislough, used to say in his cynical way that his greatest affliction was having to serve the teacher's Mass every morning. He referred, of course, to his own Mass, the curate's Mass, which was said early so that Father Fogarty could say Mass later in Costello. Nobody ever attended it, except occasionally in summer, when there were visitors at the hotel. The schoolteacher, old Considine, served as acolyte. He had been serving the early Mass long before Fogarty came, and the curate thought he would also probably be doing it long after he had left. Every morning, you saw him coming up the village street, a pedantically attired old man with a hollow face and a big moustache that was turning grey. Everything about him was abstract and angular, even to his voice, which was harsh and without modulation, and sometimes when he and Fogarty came out of the sacristy with Considine leading, carrying the book, his pace was so slow that Fogarty wondered what effect it would have if he gave him one good kick in the behind. It was exactly as Fogarty said – as though *he* were serving Considine's Mass, and the effect of it was to turn Fogarty into a more unruly acolyte than ever he had been in the days when he himself was serving the convent Mass.

Whatever was the cause, Considine always roused a bit of the devil in Fogarty, and he knew that Considine had no great affection for him, either. The old man had been headmaster of the Crislough school until his retirement, and all his life he had kept himself apart from the country people, like a parish priest or a policeman. He was not without learning; he had a quite respectable knowledge of local history, and a very good one of the ecclesiastical history of the Early Middle Ages in its local applications, but it was all book learning, and, like his wing collar, utterly unrelated to the life about him. He had all the childish vanity of the man of dissociated scholarship, wrote occasional scurrilous letters to the local paper to correct some error in etymology, and expected everyone on that account to treat him as an oracle. As a schoolmaster he had sneered cruelly at the barefoot urchins he taught, describing them as 'illiterate peasants' who believed in the fairies and in spells, and when, twenty years later, some of them came back from Boston or Brooklyn and showed off before the neighbours, with their big American hats and high-powered cars, he still sneered at them. According to him, they went away illiterate and came home illiterate.

'I see young Carmody is home again,' he would say to the curate after Mass.

'Is that so?'

'And he has a car like a house,' Considine would add, with bitter amusement. 'A car with a grin on it. 'Twould do fine to cart home his mother's turf.'

'The blessings of God on him,' the curate would say cheerfully. 'I wish I had a decent car instead of the old yoke I have.'

'I dare say it was the fairies,' the old teacher would snarl, with an ugly smile that made his hollow, high-cheeked face look like a skull. 'It wasn't anything he ever learned here.'

'Maybe we're not giving the fairies their due, Mr Considine,' said the curate, with the private conviction that it would be easier to learn from them than from the schoolmaster.

The old man's scornful remarks irritated Fogarty because he liked the wild, barefooted, inarticulate brats from the mountainy farms, and felt that if they showed off a bit when

they returned from America with a few dollars in their
pockets, they were well entitled to do so. Whoever was entitled to the credit, it was nothing and nobody at home. The
truth was he had periods of terrible gloom when he felt he
had mistaken his vocation. Or, rather, the vocation was all
right, but the conditions under which he exercised it were
all wrong, and those conditions, for him, were well represented by the factitious scholarship of old Considine. It was all
in the air. Religion sometimes seemed no more to him than
his own dotty old housekeeper, who, whatever he said, in-
vested herself with the authority of a bishop and decided
who was to see him and about what, and settled matters on
her own whenever she got half a chance. Things were so bad
with her that whenever the country people wanted to see
him, they bribed one of the acolytes to go and ask him to
come himself to their cottages. The law was represented by
Sergeant Twomey, who raided the mountain pubs half an
hour after closing time, in response to the orders of some
lunatic superintendent at the other side of the county, while
as for culture, there was the library van every couple of
months, from which Considine, who acted as librarian,
selected a hundred books, mainly for his own amusement.
He was partial to books dealing with voyages in the Congo
or Tibet ('Tibet is a very interessting country, Father'). The
books that were for general circulation he censored to make
sure there were no bad words like 'navel' in them that might
corrupt the ignorant 'peasantry'. And then he came to Fogarty and told him he had been reading a very 'interessting'
book about bird-watching in the South Seas, or something
like that.

Fogarty's own temptation was towards action and
energy, just as his depression was often no more than the
expression of his frustration. He was an energetic and
emotional man who in other circumstances would probably
have become a successful businessman. Women were less of
a temptation to him than the thought of an active

instinctual life. All he wanted in the way of a holiday was
to get rid of his collar and take a gun or rod and stand
behind the bar of a country hotel. He ran the local hurling team for what it was worth, which wasn't much,
and strayed down the shore with the boatmen or up the hills
with the poachers and poteen-makers, who all trusted him
and never tried to conceal any of their harmless misdemean-
ours from him. Once, for instance, in the late evening,
he came unexpectedly on a party of scared poteen-
makers on top of a mountain and sat down on the edge of
the hollow where they were operating their still. 'Never
mind me, lads!' he said, lighting a pipe. 'I'm not here at all.'
'Sure we know damn well you're not here, Father,' one old
man said, and chuckled. 'But how the hell can we offer a
drink to a bloody ghost?'

These were his own people, the people he loved and
admired, and it was principally the feeling that he could do
little or nothing for them that plunged him into those suici-
dal fits of gloom in which he took to the bottle. When he
heard of a dance being held in a farmhouse without the
permission of the priest or the police, he said, 'The blessings
of God on them', and when a girl went and got herself with
child by one of the islanders, he said, 'More power to her
elbow!' – though he had to say these things discreetly, for
fear they should get back. But the spirit of them got back,
and the acolytes would whisper, 'Father, would you ever go
out to Dan Mike's when you have the time?' or young men
and girls would lie in wait for his car on a country road and
signal timidly to him, because the country people knew that
from him they would get either a regular blasting in a
language they understood or the loan of a few pounds to
send a girl to hospital in England so that the neighbours
wouldn't know.

Fogarty knew that in the teacher's eyes this was another
black mark against him, for old Considine could not understand how any educated man could make so little of the

cloth as to sit drinking with 'illiterate peasants' instead of
talking to a fine, well-informed man like himself about the
situation in the Far East or the relationship of the Irish dio-
ceses to the old kingdoms of the Early Middle Ages.

Then one evening Fogarty was summoned to the teacher's
house on a sick call. It only struck him when he saw it there
at the end of the village – a newish, red-brick box of a house,
with pebble dash on the front and a steep stairway up from
the front door – that it was like the teacher himself. Maisie,
the teacher's unmarried daughter, was a small, plump
woman with a face that must once have been attractive, for
it was still all in curves, with hair about it like Mona Lisa's,
though now she had lost all her freshness, and her skin was
red and hard and full of wrinkles. She had a sad smile, and
Fogarty could not resist a pang of pity for her because he
realized that she was probably another victim of Considine's
dislike of 'illiterates'. How could an 'illiterate' boy come to
a house like that, or how could the teacher's daughter go out
walking with him?

She had got the old man to bed, and he lay there with the
engaged look of a human being at grips with his destiny.
From his narrow window there was a pleasant view of the
sea road and a solitary tree by the water's edge. Beyond the
bay was a mountain, with a cap on it – the sign of bad
weather. Fogarty gave him the last sacraments, and he con-
fessed and received Communion with a devotion that
touched Fogarty in spite of himself. He stayed on with the
daughter until the doctor arrived, in case any special medi-
cines were needed. They sat in the tiny box of a front room
with a bay window and a high mahogany bookcase that
filled one whole wall. She wanted to stay and make polite
conversation for the priest, though all the time she was con-
sumed with anxiety. When the doctor left, Fogarty left with
him, and pressed Maisie's hand and told her to call on him for
anything, at any time.

Dr Mulloy was more offhand. He was a tall, handsome

young man of about Fogarty's own age. Outside, standing beside his car, he said to Fogarty, 'Ah, he might last a couple of years if he minded himself. They don't, of course. You know the way it is. A wonder that daughter of his never married.'

'How could she?' Fogarty asked in a low voice, turning to glance again at the ill-designed, pretentious little suburban house. 'He'd think her too grand for any of the boys round this place.'

'Why then, indeed, if he pops off on her, she won't be too grand at all,' said the doctor. 'A wonder an educated man like that wouldn't have more sense. Sure, he can't have anything to leave her?'

'No more than myself, I dare say,' said Fogarty, who saw that the doctor only wanted to find out how much they could pay; and he went off to summon one of the boy acolytes to take Considine's place at Mass next morning.

But the next morning when Fogarty reached the sacristy, instead of the boy he had spoken to, old Considine was waiting, with everything neatly arranged in his usual pedantic manner, and a wan old man's smile on his hollow face.

'Mr Considine!' Fogarty exclaimed indignantly. 'What's the meaning of this?'

'Ah, I'm fine this morning, Father,' said the old man, with a sort of fictitious, drunken excitement. 'I woke up as fresh as a daisy.' Then he smiled malevolently and added, 'Jimmy Leary thought he was after doing me out of a job, but Dr Mulloy was too smart for him.'

'But you know yourself what Dr Mulloy said,' Fogarty protested indignantly. 'I talked to him myself about it. He said you could live for years, but any exertion might make you go off any minute.'

'And how can man die better?' retorted the teacher, with the triumphant air he wore whenever he managed to produce an apt quotation. 'You remember Macaulay, I suppose,'

he added doubtfully, and then his face took on a morose
look. ' 'Tisn't that at all,' he said. 'But 'tis the only thing I
have to look forward to. The day wouldn't be the same to
me if I had to miss Mass.'

Fogarty knew that he was up against an old man's stub-
bornness and love of habitual things, and that he was wasting his breath advising Considine himself. Instead, he talked
to the parish priest, a holy and muddleheaded old man
named Whelan. Whelan shook his head mournfully over the
situation, but then he was a man who shook his head over
everything. He had apparently decided many years ago that
any form of action was hateful, and he took to his bed if
people became too pressing.

'He's very obstinate, old John, but at the same time, you
wouldn't like to cross him,' Whelan said.

'If you don't do something about it, you might as well put
back the Costello Mass another half an hour,' Fogarty said.
He was for ever trying to induce Whelan to make up his
mind. 'He's getting slower every day. One of these days he'll
drop dead on me at the altar.'

'Oh, I'll mention it to him,' the parish priest said regretfully. 'But I don't know would it be wise to take too
strong a line. You have to humour them when they're as
old as that. I dare say we'll be the same ourselves, Father.'

Fogarty knew he was wasting his breath on Whelan as
well. Whelan would no doubt be as good as his word, and
talk about the weather to Considine for an hour, and then
end by dropping a hint, which might be entirely lost, that
the old teacher shouldn't exert himself too much, and that
would be all.

A month later, the old teacher had another attack, but this
time Fogarty only heard of it from his mad housekeeper,
who knew everything that went on in the village.

'But why didn't he send for me?' he asked sharply.

'Ah, I suppose he wasn't bad enough,' replied the housekeeper. 'Mrs MacCarthy said he got over it with pills and a

sup of whiskey. They say whiskey is the best thing.'

'You're sure he didn't send for me?' Fogarty asked. There were times when he half expected the woman, in the exercise of her authority, to refuse the Last Rites to people she didn't approve of.

'Sure, of course he didn't. It was probably nothing.'

All the same, Fogarty was not easy in his mind. He knew what it meant to old people to have the priest with them at the end, and he suspected that if Considine made light of his attack, it could only be because he was afraid Fogarty would take it as final proof that he was not fit to serve Mass. He felt vaguely guilty about it. He strode down the village street, saluting the fishermen who were sitting on the sea wall in the dusk. The teacher's cottage was dark when he reached it. The cobbler, a lively little man who lived next door, was standing outside.

'I hear the old master was sick again, Tom,' said the curate.

'Begor, he was, Father,' said the cobbler. 'I hear Maisie found him crawling to the fire on his hands and knees. Terrible cold they get when they're like that. He's a sturdy old divil, though. You needn't be afraid you'll lose your altar boy for a long time yet.'

'I hope not, Tom,' said Fogarty, who knew that the cobbler, a knowledgeable man in his own way, thought there was something funny about the old schoolmaster's serving Mass. 'And I hope we're all as good when our own time comes.'

He went home, too thoughtful to chat with the fishermen. The cobbler's words had given him a sudden glimpse of old Considine's sufferings, and he was filled with the compassion that almost revolted him at times for sick bodies and suffering minds. He was an emotional man, and he knew it was partly the cause of his own savage gloom, but he could not restrain it.

Next morning, when he went to the sacristy, there was

the old teacher, with his fawning smile, the smile of a guilty small boy who has done it again and this time knows he will not escape without punishment.

'You weren't too good last night, John,' the curate said, using Considine's Christian name for the first time.

'No, Father Jeremiah,' Considine replied, pronouncing the priest's name slowly and pedantically. 'I was a bit poorly in the early evening. But those pills of Dr Mulloy's are a wonder.'

'And isn't it a hard thing to say you never sent for me?' Fogarty went on.

Considine blushed furiously, and this time he looked really guilty and scared.

'But I wasn't that bad, Father,' he protested with senile intensity, his hands beginning to shake and his eyes to sparkle. 'I wasn't as frightened yesterday as I was the first time. It's the first time it frightens you. You feel sure you'll never last it out. But after that you get to expect it.'

'Will you promise me never to do a thing like that again?' the curate asked earnestly. 'Will you give me your word that you'll send for me, any hour of the day or night?'

'Very well, Father,' Considine replied sullenly. ' 'Tis very good of you. I'll give you my word I'll send for you.'

And they both recognized the further, unspoken part of the compact between them. Considine would send for Fogarty, but nothing Fogarty saw or heard was to permit him again to try to deprive the old teacher of his office. Not that he any longer wished to do so. Now that he recognized the passion of will in the old man, Fogarty's profound humanity only made him anxious to second it and enable Considine to do what clearly he wished to do – die in harness. Fogarty had also begun to recognize that it was not mere obstinacy that got the old man out of his bed each morning and brought him shivering and sighing and shuffling up the village street. There was obstinacy there, and plenty of it, but there was something else, which the curate valued more;

something he felt the lack of in himself. It wasn't easy to put a name on it. Faith was one name, but it was no more than a name and was used to cover too many excesses of devotion that the young priest found distasteful. This was something else, something that made him ashamed of his own human weakness and encouraged him to fight the depression, which seemed at times as if it would overwhelm him. It was more like the miracle of the Mass itself, metaphor become reality. Now when he thought of his own joke about serving the teacher's Mass, it didn't seem quite so much like a joke.

One morning in April, Fogarty noticed as he entered the sacristy that the old man was looking very ill. As he helped Fogarty, his hands shook piteously. Even his harsh voice had a quaver in it, and his lips were pale. Fogarty looked at him and wondered if he shouldn't say something, but decided against it. He went in, preceded by Considine, and noticed that though the teacher tried to hold himself erect, his walk was little more than a shuffle. He went up to the altar, but found it almost impossible to concentrate on what he was doing. He heard the labouring steps behind him, and as the old man started to raise the heavy book on to the altar, Fogarty paused for a moment and looked under his brows. Considine's face was now white as a sheet, and as he raised the book he sighed. Fogarty wanted to cry out, 'For God's sake, man, lie down!' He wanted to hold Considine's head on his knee and whisper into his ear. Yet he realized that to the strange old man behind him this would be no kindness. The only kindness he could do him was to crush down his own weak warmheartedness and continue the Sacrifice. Never had he seemed further away from the reality of the Mass. He heard the labouring steps, the panting breath, behind him, and it seemed as if they had lasted some timeless time before he heard another heavy sigh as Considine managed to kneel.

At last, Fogarty found himself waiting for a response that

did not come. He looked round quickly. The old man had fallen silently forward on to the altar steps. His arm was twisted beneath him and his head was turned sideways. His jaw had fallen, and his eyes were sightless.

'John!' Fogarty called, in a voice that rang through the church. 'Can you hear me? John!'

There was no reply, and the curate placed him on his back, with one of the altar cushions beneath his head. Fogarty felt under the surplice for his buttons and unloosed them. He felt for the heart. It had stopped; there was no trace of breathing. Through the big window at the west end he saw the churchyard trees and the sea beyond them, bright in the morning light. The whole church seemed terribly still, so that the mere ticking of the clock filled it with its triumphant mocking of the machine of flesh and blood that had fallen silent.

Fogarty went quickly to the sacristy and returned with the Sacred Oils to anoint the teacher. He knew he had only to cross the road for help, to have the old man's body removed and get an acolyte to finish the Mass, but he wanted no help. He felt strangely lightheaded. Instead, when he had done, he returned to the altar and resumed the Mass where he had left off, murmuring the responses to himself. As he did so, he realized that he was imitating the harsh voice of Considine. There was something unearthly about it, for now the altar which had seemed so far away was close to him, and though he was acutely aware of every detail, of every sound, he had no feeling that he was lacking in concentration. When he turned to face the body of the church and said, '*Dominus vobiscum*', he saw as if for the first time the prostrate form with its fallen jaw and weary eyes, under the light that came in from the sea through the trees in their first leaf, and murmured, '*Et cum spiritu tuo*' for the man whose spirit had flown. Then, when he had said the prayers after Mass beside the body, he took his biretta, donned it, and walked by the body, carrying his chalice, and feeling as he walked that some figure was walking before him, slowly, saying goodbye. In his excited mind echoed the rubric: 'Then, having adored and thanked God for everything, he goes away.'

(1955)

ANCHORS

IT was always a mystery to me how anyone as rational as myself came of parents so befuddled. Sometimes it was as if I lived on a mountain-peak away up in the sunlight while they fumbled and squabbled in a valley below. Except for a tendency to quarrel violently about politics, Father was not so bad. At least, there were things I could talk to him about, but Mother was a constant source of irritation to me as well as to him.

She was a tall, thin, mournful woman, with beautiful blue eyes and a clear complexion, but harassed by hard work and piety. She had lost her second child in childbirth, and, having married late so that she was incapable of having further children, she tended to brood over it. She had no method, and was always losing a few shillings on the horses, borrowing to make it up so that Father wouldn't know, and then taking sips of whiskey on the side to nerve her for the ordeal of confessing it to him. She was in and out of churches all day, trying to pump the sly ones who had friends in the priesthood for inside information about saints who were free of their favours. At any time a few pounds would have made her solvent again, and a favour like that would be nothing to a saint. If she worried over the souls of Father and me, that was pure kindness of heart, because she had quite enough to do, worrying about herself.

Her brand of religion really got under my skin. As I say, I was a natural rationalist. Even as a young fellow, all my sympathies were with the labour movement, and I had

nothing but amused contempt for the sort of faction-fighting
that Father and his contemporaries mistook for politics. I
had an intensely orderly mind, and had no difficulty in
working out a technique to keep myself near the head of the
class in school. But nothing would convince Mother but that
you passed examinations by the aid of the Infant Jesus of
Prague and St Rose of Lima. She was a plain woman who
regarded Heaven as a glorified extension of the Cork County
Council and the saints as elected representatives whose duty
it was to attend to the interests of the constituents and relatives. In religion, education, and business the principle of the
open competitive examination simply did not exist for
Mother. People might say what they liked, but 'pull' was the
thing. Naturally, in the manner of elected representatives
the world over, the saints were a mixed lot. Some were smar-
ter or more conscientious than others; some promised more
than they could perform, while others had never been any
good to anyone, and it was folly to rely on them. You had to
study form as though they were horses, and, apart from the
racing column, the only thing that interested Mother in the
evening paper was the chain of acknowledgements of
'favours received on promise of publication'. From this,
anyone could see that the Infant Jesus of Prague and St Rose
of Lima left the rest of the field behind. Hard work might be
all right in its own place; brilliance might do some good if it
didn't get you into trouble; but examinations were passed by
faith rather than good works.

It was a subtle sort of insult to which I was particularly
sensitive, though, of course, I never let on. I had trained
myself with the foolish people in school to be silent, and the
most I ever permitted myself when I was riled was a sniff or
a smile. I had discovered that this made them much
madder.

'You'd never imagine the saints would be so keen to get
into the papers,' I said one evening when she insisted on
reading it aloud.

'Musha, why wouldn't they?' she asked, showing her teeth in a smile. 'I suppose they're as glad to be told they're appreciated as the rest of us.'

'Oh, I dare say,' I said lightly, 'but you wouldn't think they'd be so mad on publicity.'

'And how would people know?' she asked timidly. 'Look at this young fellow, for instance. He passed an examination the fourth time after praying to St Rose.'

'Maybe he'd have passed it the first time without praying to anybody if he did his work,' I suggested.

'Ah,' she said, 'everybody can't be smart.'

'But why worry to be smart?' I asked, getting more supercilious than ever. 'Why worry to do anything? You ought to try out your method on someone else.'

'How do you mean, on someone else?'

'Well, working on me, you're never going to find out the truth about it. You should try it on someone who needs it. There's a fellow in my class called Mahony who could do with someone's prayers.'

'Why then, indeed, I'll pray for the poor boy if you want me to.'

'Do,' I said encouragingly. 'We'll see how it works out. But you'll have to leave me out of your prayers, or we'll never get it straight.'

'Why, then, what a thing I'd do!' she retorted with real indignation.

My father never interfered in these discussions, except for an occasional snort of amusement at some impertinence of mine, and, for all the apparent interest he took in them, might as well not have been listening. He was a tall, gaunt man with a haunted look, and it seemed to me that he was haunted by the revolutionary politics of his generation. In so far as the Church had opposed the revolution and distorted its aims, he was violently anti-clerical, particularly when it was a question of Father Dempsey, the parish priest. Dempsey was a fat, coarse, jolly man, and he had made fun

of Father when Father had called on him to arrange for
Masses for the souls of some revolutionary friends of his. I
did not think much of Father's generation or of revolution-
ists who didn't see that before you dealt with the British
Empire you had first to put the Dempseys in their place.

By the time I went to the university I hadn't a shred of
belief left in St Rose of Lima or Cathleen ni Houlihan. I
thought them both fetishes of the older generation, and was
seriously considering severing my relations with the
Church. I was restrained partly by fear of the effect that this
would have on my parents, particularly my father, and
partly because I could see nothing to put in its place. I didn't
have to look far to see that man was prone to evil. I knew
well that for all my reasonableness I had a violent temper
and brutal appetites. I knew that there was a streak of pos-
itive cruelty in me. I could not even walk through the main
street without averting my eyes from the shop windows
that displayed women's underclothing, and sometimes it
drove me mad with rage because I knew that the owners and
their staffs were supposed to be pious Catholics. I had begun
walking out with a girl called Babiche, which made it even
worse, because she was interested in underclothing. She
thought I was a queer coon, and no wonder. Little did she
know of the passions that raged in me.

But in the battle between fear of the evil in myself and
sheer boredom with the superstitions of people like Mother,
boredom had it, and I knew I must express this in action. It
was not enough to believe something; I had to show that I
believed it. Now there was nothing between myself and
avowed agnosticism but fear of the effect it would have on
my parents.

Father and I usually went to Mass together, not to the
parish church where he might be submitted to the ordeal of
listening to Father Dempsey, but to the Franciscan church in
Sheares Street, where he had gone to get his Masses said and
where they hadn't laughed at him. Father was not a man

to forget a kindness. After Mass we usually took a walk up the tree-lined Mardyke, over Wellington Bridge, and back through the expensive suburb of Sunday's Well. There were beautiful houses along the way, and Father knew who had built them and never tired of admiring them. I enjoyed those walks, the hillside of Sunday's Well seen under the trees of the Dyke, the river by the tramstop, and the great view of the city from the top of Wyse's Hill, but mainly Father's company because these were the only occasions when we were alone together and I could talk to him.

One Sunday in spring as we went up the Dyke I decided to break the bad news to him.

'You know, Dad, there's something I wanted to tell you,' I said, and realized the moment I had said it that I had begun badly. Father started and frowned. If you wanted to get at Father you had to prepare him beforehand, as you prepare an audience in the theatre for the hero's death. Mother never prepared him for anything, seeing that she never told him anything until she had herself broken down, and as a result she nearly always provoked the wrong reaction.

'What's that?' he snapped suspiciously.

'Oh, just that I don't think I can come to Mass with you any more,' I said, trying to make myself sound casual.

'Why not?' he asked angrily.

'Well,' I said deliberately, trying to make it sound as though I were full of grief about it, 'I don't know that I believe in God any more.'

'You what?' he asked, stopping dead and looking at me out of the corner of his eye. It was the reaction I had feared, the spontaneous reaction of a man who has been told that his wife is betting again.

'I'm sorry, Dad,' I said reasonably. 'I was afraid it would upset you, but at the same time I felt you ought to be told.'

Father drew a deep breath through his nose as though to indicate that I had a very lighthearted attitude to his feelings, gave me another look out of the corner of his eye and reached for his pipe. He went behind a tree to light it and walked on again, puffing at it. Then he sucked his lips in a funny way he had and grinned at me.

'I was afraid you were going to tell me something serious,' he said.

I smiled. At the same time I was surprised and suspicious. I knew he was lacking in Mother's brand of religiosity, but I had not expected this particular tone and had no confidence in it.

'It seems serious enough to me,' I said.

'You're sure 'tis God you don't believe in?' he asked roguishly. 'Not Dempsey by any chance?'

'I can't very well pretend I don't believe in the existence of Dempsey,' I said with a smile.

'It's a very important distinction,' he said gravely. 'One is anti-clericalism, a view taken only by the most religious people – myself, for instance. The other is atheism, a view held by – ah, a lot of people who are also deeply religious. You'd want to be sure you don't get in the wrong camp.'

'You think the anti-clerical camp would be good enough for me?' I asked.

'I wouldn't get things mixed up if I were you,' he said, growing serious again. 'People are only what society makes them, you know. You might think you were against religion when all you were against was a lot of scared old women. Country towns are bad that way. Religion is something more than that.'

'I'm not sure I know what you mean by religion,' I said, trying to steer him into one of my favourite arguments, but he wasn't having any.

'Ah, 'tisn't what I mean by religion, boy,' he replied testily. 'The best brains in the world are at that for thousands of years, and you talk as I was just after making it up.'

'Well, I've only been at it for six months,' I said reasonably, 'so I have time enough. What do you think I ought to do?'

'I think you ought to make sure what you're giving up before you do it,' he said. 'I don't want you coming to me in six months' time and telling me about some astounding discovery you could have made in a penny catechism. You know, of course, a thing like that will come against you if you're looking for a job.'

'You think it would?' I asked in some surprise. There were still a lot of things I did not know about life.

'I'm damn sure it would,' he said with a little snarl of amusement. 'If you think I'm ever likely to get a church to build you're mistaken. But that's neither here nor there. If you felt like that about it I wouldn't try to stop you.'

'I know that,' I said affectionately. 'That's why I didn't want to do anything without asking your advice.'

'Oh, my advice!' he sniffed. 'I'm not a proper person to advise you. Get hold of some intelligent young priest of about your own age and get him to advise you. And there's a few books you could read.'

Now, this was the first I had heard of religious books in the home, apart from some detestable tracts that Mother had bought. Father searched them out from a pile of old papers in the lumber-room; newspapers, pamphlets, election hand-bills, and broadsheet ballads – Father's wild oats. He squatted on the floor, sucking his pipe and enthusing over them. 'Begor, I never knew I had this. This would be valu-able. Look! An account of poor Jim Tracy's trial – he was shot in Cork barrack after. You ought to read that.' He had lost all interest in the books by the time he found them – a couple of volumes of Newman, a handbook of dogmatic the-ology and a study of Thomas Aquinas. It was a side of Father I'd never known. It was a side that didn't seem too familiar to Father himself, either, for he raised his brows over pages he had underlined and scored along the margins. As he read the marked passages he nodded a couple of times, but it was a puzzled sort of nod. He seemed uneasy and anxious to get back to more familiar surroundings.

However, it was all I needed, and it quieted the tumult in my mind. I had fancied myself so much alone, and it was a relief to know that others I could respect had shared my doubts. Church services that had left me bored took on a new interest for me. It was pleasant to be able to explain details of the rubrics to Babiche, who knew as little of them as I had known.

The result was a new wave of fervour, different from any I had known as a kid. I had always been a bit of a busybody and enjoyed helping and protecting other people, but because I had been afraid of being thought a sissy, I had concealed it. Now that I had found another source of strength outside myself, I was able to dispense with my fears. I need no longer be ashamed of coming up the road with one raggy kid riding my neck and another swinging from my arm.

And because Mother had always been such a sore trial to me, I felt I must be especially kind to her, even to the point of taking her side against Father. I rose at seven each morning, lit the fire, and brought herself and Father their tea in bed. I stayed around the house in my free hours to keep her company and do the odd jobs that Father could never be induced to do for her. I had never realized before what a tough life she had had of it; how awkward was the kitchen where she had to work, and how few comforts there were for her. I even went to the point of making an armchair for her, since when Father was in she had none of her own.

Now, anyone would assume that a pious woman like Mother would have been delighted to see her godless son turn suddenly into a walking saint. Not a bit of it. The more virtuous I became, the gloomier she got. Only gradually did it dawn on me that she did not approve of men saving their own souls, since, like cooking and laundry, this was something that could only be done for them by their womenfolk. A man who tried to do if for himself was no man at all.

'Is there anything I can get you in town?' I would ask, and she would smile mournfully at me with her fine set of false teeth.

'Ah, no, child. What would you get?'

'Oh, I just wondered if there were any messages.'

'And if there are, can't I do them myself? I'm not too old for that, am I?'

I was studying for my final at the time and she was in a frenzy, working on St Rose. As part of my new character I let her be, contenting myself with suggesting saints who were in some way related to culture – St Finnbarr, for instance, the supposed founder of the college, or St Thomas Aquinas. She had heard of St Finnbarr as patron of the Protestant cathedral, so she refused point-blank to have anything to do with him. She didn't dispute the man's orthodoxy, but it wouldn't be lucky. She didn't like to commit herself on the subject of St Thomas, who might, for all she knew, be quite decent, but by this time she was convinced that I was only making up saints to annoy her.

'Who was he?' she asked without any great confidence.

'Well, he happened to be the greatest intellect of the Church,' I said sweetly.

'Was it he wrote that old book you were reading?'

'No, that was G. K. Chesterton – a different family altogether.'

'Wouldn't you think if he was so great that someone would hear about him?'

Father gave a snort and went out to the front door. As I passed out he gave me one of his sideways looks.

'I'd try the African Mission,' he said.

'Funny the different forms religion takes,' I said, standing beside him with my hands in my pockets.

'Religion?' he repeated. 'You don't call that religion? No woman has any religion.'

As usual I felt that he was exaggerating for the sake of effect, but I had to admit that whatever religion Mother had was not of an orthodox kind. At the time I was deeply concerned with the problem of faith as against good works, but with her the problem simply didn't arise. She was just then going through a crisis on the subject of a new apparition that had taken place in County Kerry, and had succeeded in laying hold of a bottle of water from a holy well where the Blessed Virgin and a number of saints had appeared. The half of Ireland was making pilgrimages to the spot, and what made it all more mysterious was that the newspapers were not allowed by the Church authorities to refer to it in any way. I made inquiries and discovered that the apparitions had taken place on the farm of a well-known poteenmaker whose trade had fallen on evil days; that the police had searched every electrical shop for miles around in hopes of tracing batteries for a large magic lantern, and that there was no well on the farm. At the same time she was very excited by the report that Father Dempsey had performed a miraculous cure on a child with diphtheria, though, according to Mother's brand of Catholicism, this meant he had taken the disease on himself, and she was now anxiously waiting till he succumbed to it.

I kept on preaching sound doctrine on such matters to her with no great effect. But I did not grow alarmed for her till some weeks later. As I say, she had never got over the loss of her second child. In fact, she had created a sort of fantasy life for him into which she retreated whenever the horses became more incalculable than usual. She had nursed him through various childish ailments, sent him to school, and seen him through college. He had no clear outline in her mind except the negative one of not resembling me. *He* passed his examinations entirely through the power of her prayers. Naturally, he had shown a vocation from the earliest age, and I strongly suspect that for a great part of the time he was a bishop or archbishop who put manners on the raw young priests her supercilious cronies took such pride in. I had heard about him so often that I didn't attach any great importance to the matter. It was only as a result of my own reading that I began to see its doctrinal significance and realized that Mother was a heretic. I remonstrated with her, mildly enough at first, but, for all the difference it made to her, I could have been speaking of the poteen-maker's apparitions. She had accustomed herself to the thought of my brother's waiting for her in Heaven, and she continued to see him there, regardless of anything I said. As usual, Father said nothing.

'Ah, well,' she said one evening when I was having tea, 'it won't be so long till I see your brother again, please God.'

'Father and I needn't worry much about you so,' I said.

'Wisha, what do you mean, child?' she asked in alarm.

'You'll have an awful long time to wait if you're waiting for that,' I said, pleasantly enough, as I thought. 'You'll see both of us under the sod.' Then, as I saw her gaping at me, I added, 'I only mean that he can't very well be in Heaven.'

'Musha, what nonsense you're talking!' she exclaimed roughly, though at the same time she was disturbed. 'Is it an innocent child?'

'I suppose you'll tell me next you never heard of Original Sin?' I asked.

'Ah, for all the sin my poor child had on him!' she sighed. 'Where else would he be, only in Heaven, the little angel!'

'The Church says he's in Limbo,' I said cheerfully, taking another mouthful of bacon.

'The Church does?'

'Yes.'

'In Limbo?'

'That's what we're supposed to believe.'

'Pisherogues!' she said angrily.

My father got up and strode to the front door with his hands in his trouser pockets. I controlled myself as best I could at her unmannerly reference to the doctrine of Original Sin as fairytales. It didn't come too well from a woman who had just been telling us of a priest that died suddenly after seeing the Holy Ape on the poteen-maker's property.

'That's what you may think,' I said coldly. 'Of course, you don't have to believe it unless you want to, but it is a fundamental dogma and you can't be a Catholic without it.'

'Pisherogues!' she repeated violently. 'I was a Catholic before they were. What do they know about it?'

'So you *do* claim the right to private judgement?' I said menacingly.

'Private what?' she asked in exasperation.

'Private judgement,' I repeated. 'Of course, you'll find a lot of people to agree with you, but you'd better realize that you're speaking as a Protestant.'

'Are you mad?' she asked, half rising from her chair at the implication that there was anything in common between her and the poor unenlightened souls who attended St Finnibarr's.

'Isn't it true that you won't believe anything only what suits yourself?' I asked patiently.

'Listen to him, you sweet God!' Mother moaned. 'I only believe what suits me! Me that have the knees wore off myself praying for him! You pup!' she added in what for her was a flash of real anger.

'But that's exactly what you do,' I said gently, ignoring her abuse. 'You believe things that no one ever asked you to believe. You believe in the poteen-maker's apparitions and his holy well, and Dempsey's diphtheria cure, but you won't believe the essential teaching of the Church whenever it disagrees with your own foolish notions. What sort of religion is that?'

'Ah,' she said, almost weeping with rage, 'I was practising my religion before you were born. And my mother before me. Oh, you pup, to talk like that to me!'

I sighed and shrugged and left the house. I was more upset than I let on to be. I had seen her in plenty of states before, but never so angry and bewildered. I had a date with Babiche by the bridge, and we went up the hills together in the direction of a wood that was a favourite haunt of ours. I told her the whole story, making fun of it as I did so. After all, it was funny. Here had I been on the point of cutting loose from religion altogether because of my family, and now that I had really got back the faith it was only to discover that my own home was a nest of heretics.

It struck me that Babiche was not taking it in the spirit in which I offered it. Usually, she made no attempt to follow up an argument, but caught at some name or word like 'Athanasius' or 'Predestination' and then repeated it for months with joyous inconsequence and in contexts with which it had nothing whatever to do. This evening she seemed to be angry and argumentative as well.

'That was a nice thing to say to your mother,' she snapped.

'What was wrong with it?' I asked in surprise.

'Plenty. You weren't the kid's mother. She was.'

'Now, really, Babiche,' I protested, 'what has that to do with it? I suppose I was his brother, but that's neither here nor there.'

'A dead kid is neither here nor there,' she said sullenly. 'You don't care. You're only delighted to have a brother in Limbo, or wherever the blazes it is. It's like having one in the Civil Service. If you had another you could say was in Hell you'd feel you were made for life.'

I was taken aback. I knew Babiche was unjust, and I realized that Father was right and that no woman in the world had any religion whatever, but at the same time I felt I might have gone too far. I did tend to take my own line firmly and go on without considering how other people might feel about it. We were sitting in a clearing above the wood, looking down at the river winding through the valley in the evening light. I put out my hand, but Babiche pulled her own hand away.

'I'm sorry, Babiche,' I said apologetically. 'I didn't mean to start a row.'

Then she grinned and gave me back her hand, and in no time we were embracing. Babiche was anything but a profound thinker, above all when someone was making love to her. I found myself making love to her as I'd never done before, and she enjoyed it. Then she looked away towards the city and began to laugh.

'What's the joke?' I asked.

'If I have a kid like that, and you start telling me he's in Limbo, I'll scratch your eyes out,' she said.

This time I felt really guilty towards Mother. But worse than that, the wild beast in me was in danger of breaking out again. It was horrible. You swung from instinct to judgement, and from judgement back to instinct, and nothing ever seemed to arrest the pendulum.

But next morning when I woke the sun was shining through the attic window, and I lay watching it, feeling that something very peculiar had happened to me. I didn't yet know what it was, but I realized that it was very pleasant. I felt fine. Then it all became clear. The pendulum had stopped. I had lost my faith, and this time I had lost it for good. My brother might not be in Heaven, but I was sure he wasn't in Limbo either. I didn't believe in Limbo. It was too silly. The previous months of exultation and anxiety seemed like a nightmare. Nor was I in the least afraid of the beast in myself because I knew now that whatever happened I should always care too much for Babiche to injure her. Anyone who really cared for human beings need never be afraid of either conscience or passion.

The following Sunday when Father and I reached the church door I stopped and smiled at him.

'I'll see you after Mass, Dad,' I said.

Father showed no surprise, but he paused before replying in a businesslike tone: 'I think we'll go down the Marina for a change. We weren't down there this year.'

I was heartsick at his disappointment and the brave way he kept his word. That was one thing to be said for the older generation: they knew the meaning of principle.

'You know the way I feel about it?' I said, squaring up and looking at him.

'What's that?' he asked sharply. 'Oh, yes,' he added, 'we all go through it. You have time enough . . . Tell me, who's that little black-haired girl you're knocking round with?'

'Babiche Regan?' I asked, surprised that he knew so much.

'Is she one of the Regans of Sunday's Well?'

'That's right,' I replied, a bit mystified.

'They're a very good family,' Father said approvingly. 'I used to know her father on the County Council. Is she a fancy or a regular?'

'Well,' I said, shrugging my shoulders in embarrassment, 'I suppose I'll be marrying her one of these days.'

'Good man! Good man!' he said with a nod. 'Ah, well, by the time you're settled down, you'll know your own mind better . . . Now, don't be late for that walk.'

I went up the Mardyke in its summer-morning calm, a free man for the first time. But I didn't feel free. There was something about Father's tone that had disturbed me. It was as though he expected Babiche to turn out like Mother and me like himself. It was hardly possible, of course: even he couldn't believe that Babiche would ever prove so irrational or I so weak. But all the same I was disturbed.

(1952)

THE PARTY

OLD JOHNNY, one of the Gas Company's watchmen, was a man with a real appreciation of his job. Most of the time, of course, it was a cold, comfortless job, with no one to talk to, and he envied his younger friend Tim Coakley, the postman. Postmen had a cushy time of it – always watched and waited for, bringing good news or bad news, often called in to advise, and (according to Tim, at least) occasionally called in for more intimate purposes. Tim, of course, was an excitable man, and he could be imagining a lot of that, though Johnny gave him the benefit of the doubt. At the same time, queer things happened to Johnny now and again that were stranger than anything Tim could tell. As it seemed to Johnny, people got it worse at night; the wild ones grew wilder, the gloomy ones gloomier. Whatever it was in them that had light in it burned more clearly, the way the stars and moon did when the sun went down. It was the darkness that did it. Johnny would be sitting in his hut for hours in the daylight and no one even gave him a second glance, but once darkness fell, people would cross the street to look at his brazier, and even stop to speak to him.

One night, for instance, in the week before Christmas, he was watching in a big Dublin square, with a railed-off park in the middle of it and doctors' and lawyers' houses on all the streets about it. That suited Johnny fine, particularly at that time of year, when there was lots of visiting and entertaining. He liked to be at the centre of things, and he always appreciated the touch of elegance: the stone steps leading up to the tall door, with the figures entering and leaving looking small in the lighted doorway, and the slight voices echoing on the great brick sounding-board of the square.

One house in particular attracted him. It was all lit up as if for a party, and the curtains were pulled back to reveal the tall, handsome rooms with decorated plaster ceilings. A boy with a basket came and rang, and a young man in evening dress leaned out of the window and told the boy to leave the stuff in the basement. As he did so, a girl came and rested her hand on his shoulder, and she was in evening dress too. Johnny liked that. He liked people with a bit of style. If he had had the good fortune to grow up in a house like that, he would have done the right thing too. And even though he hadn't, it pleased him to watch the show. Johnny, who came of a generation before trade unions, knew that in many ways it is pleasanter to observe than to participate. He only hoped there would be singing; he was very partial to a bit of music.

But this night a thing happened the like of which had never happened to Johnny before. The door of the house opened and closed, and a man in a big cloth coat like fur came across the road to him. When he came closer, Johnny saw that he was a tall, thin man with greying hair and a pale discontented face.

'Like to go home to bed for a couple of hours?' the man asked in a low voice.

'What's that?' said Johnny, in astonishment.

'I'll stay here and mind your box.'

'Oh, you would, would you?' Johnny said, under the impression that the man must have drink taken.

'I'm not joking,' said the man shortly.

The grin faded on Johnny's face, and he hoped God would direct him to say the right thing. This could be dangerous. It suggested only one thing – a check-up – though in this season of goodwill you'd think people would be a bit more charitable, even if a man had slipped away for a few minutes for a drink. But that was the way of bosses everywhere. Even Christmas wasn't sacred to them. Johnny put on an appearance of great sternness. 'Oho,' he said. 'I can't afford to do things like that. There's valuable property here belonging to the Gas Company. I could lose my job over a thing like that.'

'You won't lose your job,' the man said. 'I won't leave here till you come back. If there's any trouble about it, I'll get you another job. I suppose it's money you want.'

'I never asked you for anything,' Johnny replied indignantly. 'And I can't go home at this hour, with no bus to bring me back.'

'I suppose there's other places you can go,' the man replied. 'There's a quid, and I won't expect you till two.'

The sight of the money changed Johnny's view of the matter. If a rich man wanted to amuse himself doing Johnny's job for a while – a little weakness of rich men that Johnny had heard of in other connexions – and was willing to pay for it, that was all right. Rich men had to have their little jokes. Or of course, it could be a bet.

'Oh, well,' he said, rising and giving himself a shake, 'so long as there's no harm in it!' He hadn't seen the man go into the house where they were having a party, so he must live there. 'I suppose it's a joke?' he added, looking at the man out of the corner of his eye.

'It's no joke to me,' the man said gloomily.

'Oh, I wasn't being inquisitive, of course,' Johnny said hastily. 'But I see there was to be a party in the house. I thought it might be something to do with that.'

'There's your quid,' said the man. 'You needn't be back till three unless you want to. I won't get much sleep anyway.'

Johnny thanked him profusely and left in high good humour. He foresaw that the man would probably be of great use to him some time. A man who could offer to get you a job just like that was not to be slighted. And besides he had an idea of how he was going to spend the next hour or

so, at least, and a very pleasant way it was. He took a bus to
Ringstead to the house of Tim Coakley, the postman. Tim,
though a good deal younger, was very friendly with him,
and he was an expansive man who loved any excuse for a
party.

As Johnny expected, Tim, already on his way to bed, welcomed him with his two arms out and a great shout of
laughter. He was bald and fat, with a high-pitched voice.
Johnny showed Tim and his wife the money, and announced
that he was treating them to a dozen of stout. Like the
decent man he was, Tim didn't want to take the money for
the stout from Johnny, but Johnny insisted. 'Wait till I tell
you, man!' he said triumphantly. 'The like of it never happened before in the whole history of the Gas Company.'

As Johnny told the story, it took close on half an hour,
though this included Mrs Coakley's departure and return
with the dozen of stout. And then the real pleasure began,
because the three of them had to discuss what it all meant.
Why was the gentleman in the big coat sitting in the cold of
the square looking at the lights and listening to the noise of
the party in his own home? It was a real joy to Johnny to
hear his friend analyse it, for Tim had a powerful intellect,
full of novel ideas, and in no time what had begun as a
curious incident in a watchman's life was beginning to
expand into a romance, a newspaper case. Tim at once ruled
out the idea of a joke. What would be the point in a joke like
that? A bet was the more likely possibility. It could be that
the man had bet someone he could take the watchman's
place for the best part of the night without being detected,
but in Tim's view there was one fatal flaw in this explanation. Why would the man wear a coat as conspicuous
as the one that Johnny had described? There would be big
money on a wager like that, and the man would be bound to
try and disguise himself better. No, there must be another
explanation, and as Tim drank more stout, his imagination
played over the theme with greater audacity and logic, till

Johnny himself began to feel uncomfortable. He began to perceive that it might be a more serious matter than he had thought.

'We've agreed that it isn't a joke,' said Tim, holding up one finger. 'We've agreed that it isn't a bet,' he added, holding up another finger. 'There is only one explanation that covers the whole facts,' he said, holding up his open hand. 'The man is watching the house.'

'Watching his own house?' Johnny asked incredulously.

'Exactly. Why else would he pay you good money to sit in your box? A man like that, that could go to his club and be drinking champagne and playing cards all night in the best of company? Isn't it plain that he's doing it only to have cover?'

'So 'twould seem,' said Johnny meekly, like any interlocutor of Socrates.

'Now, the next question is: who is he watching?' said Tim.

'Just so,' said Johnny with a mystified air.

'So we ask ourselves: who would a man like that be watching?' Tim went on triumphantly.

'Burglars,' said Mrs Coakley.

'Burglars?' her husband asked with quiet scorn. 'I suppose they'd walk in the front door?'

'He might be watching the cars, though,' Johnny said. 'There's a lot of them young hooligans around, breaking into cars. I seen them.'

'Ah, Johnny, will you have sense?' Tim asked wearily. 'Look, if that was all the man wanted, couldn't he give you a couple of bob to keep an eye on the cars? For the matter of that, couldn't he have a couple of plainclothesmen round the square? Not at all, man! He's watching somebody, and what I say is, the one he's watching is his own wife.'

'His wife?' Johnny exclaimed, aghast. 'What would he want to watch his wife for?'

'Because he thinks someone is going to that house tonight that should not be there. Someone that wouldn't come at all unless he knew the husband was out. So what does the husband do? He pretends to go out, but instead of that he hides in a watchman's box across the road and waits for him. What other explanation is there?'

'Now, couldn't it be someone after his daughter?' said Johnny.

'What daughter?' Tim asked, hurt at Johnny's lack of logic. 'What would a well-to-do man like that do if his daughter was going with a fellow he considered unsuitable? First, he would give the daughter a clock in the jaw, and then he would say to the maid or butler or whoever he have, "If a Mr Murphy comes to this house again looking for Miss Alice, kindly tell him she is not at home." That's all he'd do, and that would be the end of your man. No, Johnny, the one he's watching is the wife, and I can only hope it won't get you into any trouble.'

'You don't think I should tell the bobbies about it?' Johnny asked in alarm.

'What *could* you tell the bobbies, though?' Tim asked. 'That there was a man in your box that paid you a quid to let him use it? What proof have you that a crime is going to be committed? None! And this is only suspicion. There's nothing you can do now, only let things take their course till two o'clock, and then I'll go round with you and see what really happened.'

'But what could happen?' Johnny asked irritably.

'He sounds to me like a desperate man,' Tim said gravely.

'Oh, desperate entirely,' agreed his wife, who was swallowing it all like a box of creams.

'You don't mean you think he might do him in?' asked Johnny.

'Him, or the wife, Johnny,' said Tim. 'Or both. Of course, it's nothing to do with you what he does,' he added comfortingly. 'Whatever it is, you had neither hand, act, nor part in it. It is only the annoyance of seeing your name in the papers.'

'A man should never take advice from anybody,' Johnny commented bitterly, opening another bottle of stout. Johnny was not a drinking man, but he was worried. He valued his own blameless character, and he knew there were people bad enough to pretend he ought not to have left his post for a couple of hours, even at Christmas time, when everybody was visiting friends. He was not a scholar like Tim, and nobody had warned him of the desperate steps that rich men took when their wives acted flighty.

'Come on,' Tim said, putting on his coat. 'I'm coming with you.'

'Now, I don't want your name dragged into this,' Johnny protested. 'You have a family to think of, too.'

'I'm coming with you, Johnny,' Tim said in a deep voice, laying his hand on Johnny's arm. 'We're old friends, and friends stick together. Besides, as a postman, I'm more accustomed to this sort of thing than you are. You're a simple man. You might say the wrong thing. Leave it to me to answer the questions.'

Johnny was grateful and said so. He was a simple man, as Tim said, and, walking back through the sleeping town, expecting to see police cordons and dead bodies all over the place, he was relieved to have a level-headed fellow like Tim along with him. As they approached the square and their steps perceptibly slowed, Tim suggested in a low voice that Johnny should stand at the corner of the square while he himself scouted round to see if everything was all right. Johnny agreed, and stopped at the corner. Everything seemed quiet enough. There were only two cars outside the house. There were lights still burning in it, but though the windows were open, as though to clear the air, there was no sound from within. His brazier still burned bright and even

in the darkness under the trees of the park. Johnny wished
he had never left it.

He saw Tim cross to the other side of the road and go
slowly by the brazier. Then Tim stopped and said something, but Johnny could not catch the words. After a few
moments, Tim went on, turned the corner, and came back
round the square. It took him close on ten minutes, and
when he reached Johnny it was clear that something was
wrong.

'What is it?' Johnny asked in agony.

'Nothing, Johnny,' Tim said sadly. 'But do you know who
the man is?'

'Sure I told you I never saw him before,' said Johnny.

'I know him,' said Tim. 'That's Hardy that owns the big
stores in George's Street. It's his house. The man must be
worth hundreds of thousands.'

'But what about his wife, man?' asked Johnny.

'Ah, his wife died ten years ago. He's a most respectable
man. I don't know what he's doing here, but it's nothing for
you to fret about. I'm glad for everyone's sake. Goodnight,
Johnny.'

'Goodnight, Tim, and thanks, thanks!' cried Johnny, his
heart already lighter.

The Gas Company's property and his reputation were
both secure. The strange man had not killed his wife or his
wife's admirer, because the poor soul, having been dead for
ten years, couldn't have an admirer for her husband or
anyone else to kill. And now he could sit in peace by his
brazier and watch the dawn come up over the decent city of
Dublin. The relief was so sharp that he felt himself superior
to Tim. It was all very well for postmen to talk about the
interesting life they led, but they hadn't the same experi-
ences as watchmen. Watchmen might seem simple to postmen, but they had a wisdom of their own, a wisdom that
came of the silence and darkness when a man is left alone

with his thoughts, like a sailor aboard ship. Thinking of the poor man sitting like that in the cold under the stars watching a party at his own house, Johnny wondered that he could ever have paid attention to Tim. He approached his brazier smiling.

'Everything nice and quiet for you?' he asked.

'Except for some gasbag that stopped for a chat five minutes ago,' the other replied with rancour. Johnny felt rather pleased to hear Tim described as a gasbag.

'I know the very man you mean,' he said with a nod. 'He's a nice poor fellow but he talks too much. Party all over?'

'Except for one couple,' the other man said, rising from his box. 'It's no use waiting for them. They'll probably be at it till morning.'

'I dare say,' said Johnny. 'Why wouldn't you go in and have a chat with them yourself? You could do with a drink by this time, I suppose.'

'A lot they care whether I could or not,' the man said bitterly. 'All that would happen is that they'd say, "Delighted to see you, Mr Hardy," and then wait for me to go to bed.'

'Ah, now, I wouldn't say that,' said Johnny.

'I'm not asking whether you'd say it or not,' said the other savagely. 'I know it. Here I am, that paid for the party, sitting out here all night, getting my death of cold, and did my daughter or my son as much as come to the door to look for me? Did they even notice I wasn't there?'

'Oh, no, no,' Johnny said politely, talking to him as if he were a ten-year-old in a tantrum – which, in a sense, Johnny felt he was. The man might have hundreds of thousands, as Tim said, but there was no difference in the world between him and a little boy sitting out in the back on a frosty night, deliberately trying to give himself pneumonia because his younger brother had got a penny and he hadn't. It was no use being hard on a man like that. 'Children are very selfish, of course, but what you must remember is that fathers are selfish, too.'

'Selfish?' the other exclaimed angrily. 'Do you know what those two cost me between private schools and colleges? Do you know what that one party tonight cost me? As much as you'd earn in a year!'

'Oh, I know, I know!' said Johnny, holding his hands up in distress. 'I used to feel the same myself, after the wife died. I'd look at the son putting grease on his hair in front of the mirror, and I'd say to myself, "That's my grease and that's my mirror, and he's going out to amuse himself with some little piece from the lanes, not caring whether I'm alive or dead!" And daughters are worse. You'd expect more from a daughter somehow.'

'You'd expect what you wouldn't get,' the other said gloomily. 'There's that girl inside that I gave everything to, and she'd think more of some spotty college boy that never earned a pound in his life. And if I open my mouth, my children look at me as if they didn't know was I a fool or a lunatic.'

'They think you're old-fashioned, of course,' said Johnny. 'I know. But all the same you're not being fair to them. Children can be fond enough of you, only you'd never see it till you didn't care whether they were or not. That was the mistake I made. If I might have got an old woman for myself after the missis died, I'd have enjoyed myself more and seen it sooner. That's what you should do. You're a well-to-do man. You could knock down a very good time for yourself. Get some lively little piece to spend your money on who'll make a fuss over you, and then you won't be-grudge it to them so much.'

'Yes,' said the other, 'to have more of them wishing I was dead so that they could get at the rest of it.'

He strode across the street without even a goodnight, and Johnny saw the flood of light on the high steps and heard the dull thud of the big door behind him.

Sitting by his brazier, waiting for the dawn over the city square, Johnny felt very fortunate, wise, and good. If ever the man listened to what he had said, he might be very good to Johnny: he might get him a proper job as an indoor watchman; he might even give him a little pension to show his appreciation. If only he took the advice – and it might sink in after a time – it would be worth every penny of it to him. Anyway, if only the job continued for another couple of days, the man would be bound to give him a Christmas box. Five bob. Ten bob. Even a quid. It would be nothing to a man like that.

Though a realist by conviction, Johnny, too, had his dreams.

(1957)

AN OUT-AND-OUT FREE GIFT

WHEN Jimmy began to get out of hand, his father was both disturbed and bewildered. Anybody else, yes, but not Jimmy! They had always been so close! Closer, indeed, than Ned ever realized, for the perfectly correct picture he had drawn of himself as a thoughtful, considerate father who treated his son as though he were a younger brother could have been considerably expanded by his wife. Indeed, to realize how close they had been you needed to hear Celia on it, because only she knew how much of the small boy there still was in her husband.

Who, for instance, would have thought that the head of a successful business had such a passion for sugar? Yet during the war, when sugar was rationed in Ireland, Celia, who was a bit of a Jansenist, had felt herself bound to give up sugar and divide her ration between Ned and Jimmy, then quite a small boy. And, even at that, Ned continued to suffer. He did admire her self-denial, but he couldn't help feeling that so grandiose a gesture deserved a better object than Jimmy. It was a matter of scientific fact that sugar was bad for Jimmy's teeth, and anything that went wrong with Jimmy's teeth was going to cost his father money. Ned felt it unfair that in the middle of a war, with his salary frozen, Celia should inflict additional burdens on him.

Most of the time he managed to keep his dignity, though he could rarely sit down to a meal without an angry glance at Jimmy's sugar bowl. To make things harder for him, Jimmy rationed himself so that towards the end of the week he still had some sugar left, while Ned had none. As a philosopher, Ned wondered that he should resent this so deeply, but resent it he did. A couple of times, he deliberately stole a spoonful while Celia's back was turned, and the absurdity of this put him in such a frivolous frame of mind for the rest of the evening that she eventually said resignedly, 'I suppose you've been at the child's sugar again? Really, Ned, you are hopeless!' On other occasions Ned summoned up all his paternal authority and with a polite 'You don't mind, old man?' took a spoonful from under Jimmy's nose. But that took nerve and a delicate appreciation of the precise moment when Jimmy could be relied on not to cry.

Towards the end of the war, it became a matter of brute economic strength. If Jimmy wanted a bicycle lamp, he could earn it or pay up in good sugar. As Ned said, quoting from a business manual he had studied in his own youth, 'There is no such thing in business as an out-and-out free gift.' Jimmy made good use of the lesson. 'Bicycle lamp, old man?' Ned would ask casually, poising his spoon over Jimmy's sugar bowl. 'Bicycle lamp *and* three-speed gear,' Jimmy would reply firmly. 'For a couple of spoons of sugar?' his father would cry in mock indignation. 'Are you mad, boy?' They both enjoyed the game.

They could scarcely have been other than friends. There was so much of the small boy in Ned that he was sensitive to the least thing affecting Jimmy, and Jimmy would consult him about things that most small boys keep to themselves. When he was in trouble, Ned never dismissed it lightly, no matter how unimportant it seemed. He asked a great many questions and frequently reserved his decisions. He had chosen Jimmy's school himself; it was a good one for Cork, and sometimes, without informing Jimmy, he went off to the school himself and had a chat with one of the teachers. Nearly always he managed to arrange things without embarrassment or pain, and Jimmy took it for granted that his decisions were usually right. It is a wise father who can persuade his son of anything of the sort.

But now, at sixteen, Jimmy was completely out of control, and his mother had handed him over to the secular arm, and the secular arm, for all its weight, made no impression on his sullen indifference. The first sign of the change in him was the disintegration of his normally perfect manners; now he seemed to have no deference towards or consideration for anyone. Ned caught him out in one or two minor falsehoods and quoted to him a remark of his own father's that 'a lie humiliates the man who tells it, but it humiliates the one it's told to even more'. What puzzled Ned was that, at the same time, the outbreak was linked in some ways to qualities he had always liked in the boy. Jimmy was strong, and showed his strength in protecting things younger and weaker than himself. The cat regarded him as a personal enemy because he hurled himself on her the moment he saw her with a bird. At one time there had been a notice on his door that read, 'Wounded Bird. Please Keep Out'. At school his juniors worshipped him because he would stand up for them against bullies, and though Ned, in a fatherly way, advised him not to get mixed up in other people's quarrels, he was secretly flattered. He felt Jimmy was taking after him.

But the same thing that attracted Jimmy to younger and weaker boys seemed now to attract him to wasters. Outside of school, he never associated with lads he might have to look up to, but only with those his father felt a normal boy should despise. All this was summed up in his friendship with a youngster called Hogan, who was a strange mixture of spoiling and neglect, a boy who had never been young and would never be old. He openly smoked a pipe, and let on to be an authority on brands of tobacco. Ned winced when Hogan addressed him as a contemporary and tried to discuss business with him. He replied with heavy irony – something he did only when he was at a complete loss. What went on in Hogan's house when Jimmy went there he could only guess at. He suspected that the parents went out and stayed out, leaving the boys to their own devices.

At first, Ned treated Jimmy's insubordination as he had treated other outbreaks, by talking to him as an equal. He even offered him a cigarette – Jimmy had stolen money to buy cigarettes. He told him how people grew up through admiration of others' virtues, rather than through tolerance of their weaknesses. He talked to him about sex, which he suspected was at the bottom of Jimmy's trouble, and Jimmy listened politely and said he understood. Whether he did or not, Ned decided that if Hogan talked sex to Jimmy, it was a very different kind of sex.

Finally, he forbade Hogan the house and warned Jimmy against going to Hogan's. He made no great matter of it, contenting himself with describing the scrapes he had got into himself at Jimmy's age, and Jimmy smiled, apparently pleased with his unfamiliar picture of his grave and rather stately father, but he continued to steal and lie, to get bad marks and remain out late at night. Ned was fairly satisfied that he went to Hogan's, and sat there smoking, playing cards, and talking filth. He bawled Jimmy out and called him a dirty little thief and liar, and Jimmy raised his brows and looked away with a pained air, as though asking himself how long he must endure such ill-breeding. At this, Ned gave him a cuff on the ear that brought a look of hatred into Jimmy's face and caused Celia not to talk to Ned for two days. But even she gave in at last.

'Last night was the third time he's been out late this week,' she said one afternoon in her apparently unemotional way. 'You'll really have to do something drastic with him.'

These were hard words from a soft woman, but though Ned felt sorry for her, he felt even sorrier for himself. He hated himself in the part of a sergeant-major, and he blamed her for having let things go so far.

'Any notion where he has been?' he asked stiffly.

'Oh, you can't get a word out of him,' she said with a

shrug. 'Judging by his tone, I'd say Hogan's. I don't know what attraction that fellow has for him.'

'Very well,' Ned said portentously. 'I'll deal with him. But, mind, I'll deal with him in my own way.'

'Oh, I won't interfere,' she said wearily. 'I know when I'm licked.'

'I can promise you Master Jimmy will know it, too,' Ned added grimly.

At supper he said in an even tone, 'Young man, for the future you're going to be home every night at ten o'clock. This is the last time I'm going to speak to you about it.'

Jimmy, apparently under the impression that his father was talking to himself, reached for a slice of bread. Then Ned let fly with a shout that made Celia jump and paralysed the boy's hand, still clutching the bread.

'Did you hear me?'

'What's that?' gasped Jimmy.

'I said you were to be in at ten o'clock.'

'Oh, all right, all right,' said Jimmy, with a look that said he did not think any reasonable person would require him to share the house any longer with one so uncivilized. Though this look was intended to madden Ned it failed to do so, because he knew that, for all her sentimentality and high liberal principles, Celia was a woman of her word and would not interfere whenever he decided to knock that particular look off Master Jimmy's face. He knew, too, that the time was not far off; that Jimmy had not the faintest intention of obeying, and that he would be able to deal with it.

'Because I warn you, the first night you're late again I'm going to skin you alive,' he added. He was trying it out, of course. He knew that Celia hated expressions of fatherly affection like 'skin you alive', 'tan you within an inch of your life', and 'knock your head off', which, to her, were relics of a barbarous age. To his great satisfaction, she neither shuddered nor frowned. Her principles were liberal, but they were principles.

Two nights after, Jimmy was late again. Celia, while pretending to read, was watching the clock despairingly. 'Of course, he may have been delayed,' she said smoothly, but there was no conviction in her tone. It was nearly eleven when they heard Jimmy's key in the door.

'I think perhaps I'd better go to bed,' she said.

'It might be as well,' he replied pityingly. 'Send that fellow in on your way.'

He heard her in the hallway, talking with Jimmy in a level, friendly voice, not allowing her consternation to appear, and he smiled. He liked that touch of the Roman matron in her. Then there was a knock, and Jimmy came in. He was a big lad for sixteen, but he still had traces of baby fat about the rosy cheeks he occasionally scraped with Ned's razor, to Ned's annoyance. Now Ned would cheerfully have given him a whole shaving kit if it would have avoided the necessity for dealing with him firmly.

'You wanted to talk to me, Dad?' he asked, as though he could just spare a moment.

'Yes, Jimmy, I did. Shut that door.'

Jimmy gave a resigned shrug at his father's mania for privacy, but did as he was told and stood against the door, his hands joined and his chin in the air.

'When did I say you were to be in?' Ned said, looking at the clock.

'When?'

'Yes. When? At what time, if you find it so hard to understand.'

'Oh, ten,' Jimmy replied wearily.

'Ten? And what time do you make that?'

'Oh, I didn't know it was so late!' Jimmy exclaimed with an astonished look at the clock. 'I'm sorry. I didn't notice the time.'

'Really?' Ned said ironically. 'Enjoyed yourself that much?'

'Not too bad,' Jimmy replied vaguely. He was always uncomfortable with his father's irony.

'Company good?'

'Oh, all right,' Jimmy replied with another shrug.

'Where was this?'

'At a house.'

'Poor people?' his father asked in mock surprise.

'What?' exclaimed Jimmy.

'Poor people who couldn't afford a clock?'

Jimmy's indignation overflowed in stammering protest. 'I never said they hadn't a clock. None of the other fellows had to be in by ten. I didn't like saying I had to be. I didn't want them to think I was a blooming . . .' The protest expired in a heavy sigh, and Ned's heart contracted with pity and shame.

Ned, now grimly determined, pursued his inquiry. 'Neither your mother nor I want you to make a show of yourself. But you didn't answer my question. Where was this party? And don't tell me any lies, because I'm going to find out.'

Jimmy grew red and angry. 'Why would I tell you lies?'

'For the same reason you've told so many already – whatever that may be. You see, Jimmy, the trouble with people who tell lies is that you have to check everything they say. Not on your account but on theirs; otherwise, you may be unfair to them. People soon get tired of being fair, though. Now, where were you? At Hogan's?'

'You said I wasn't to go to Hogan's.'

'You see, you're still not answering my questions. Were you at Hogan's?'

'No,' Jimmy replied in a whisper.

'Word of honour?'

'Word of honour.' But the tone was not the tone of honour but of shame.

'Where were you, then?'

'Ryans'.'

The name was unfamiliar to Ned, and he wondered if Jimmy had not just invented it to frustrate any attempt at checking on his statements. He was quite prepared to hear that Jimmy didn't know where the house was. It was as bad as that.

'Ryans',' he repeated evenly. 'Do I know them?'

'You might. I don't know.'

'Where do they live?'

'Gardiner's Hill.'

'Whereabouts?'

'Near the top. Where the road comes up from Dillon's Cross, four doors down. It has a tree in the garden.' It came so pat that Ned felt sure there was such a house. He felt sure of nothing else.

'And you spent the evening there? I'm warning you for your own good. Because I'm going to find out.' There was a rasp in his voice.

'I told you I did.'

'I know,' Ned said between his teeth. 'Now you're going to come along with me and prove it.'

He rose and in silence took his hat from the hall stand and went out. Jimmy followed him silently, a pace behind. It was a moonlit night, and as they turned up the steep hill, the trees overhung a high wall on one side of the street. On the other side there were steep gardens filled with shadows.

'Where did you say this house was?'

'At the top,' Jimmy replied sullenly.

The hill stopped, the road became level, and at either side were little new suburban houses, with tiny front gardens. Near the corner, Ned saw one with a tree in front of it and stopped. There was still a light in the front room. The family kept late hours for Cork. Suddenly he felt absurdly sorry for the boy.

'You don't want to change your mind?' he asked gently. 'You're sure this is where you were?'

'I told you so,' Jimmy replied almost in exasperation.

'Very well,' Ned said savagely. 'You needn't come in.'

'All right,' Jimmy said, and braced himself against the concrete gatepost, looking over the moonlit roofs at the clear sky. In the moonlight he looked very pale; his hands were drawn back from his sides, his lips drawn back from his teeth, and for some reason his white anguished face made Ned think of a crucifixion.

Anger had taken the place of pity in him. He felt the boy was being unjust towards him. He wouldn't have minded the injustice if he'd ever been unjust to Jimmy, but two minutes before he had again shown his fairness and given Jimmy another chance. Besides, he didn't want to make a fool of himself.

He walked up the little path to the door, whose coloured-glass panels glowed in light that seemed to leak from the sitting-room door. When he rang, a pretty girl of fifteen or sixteen came out and screwed up her eyes at him.

'I hope you'll excuse my calling at this unnatural hour,' Ned said in a bantering tone. 'It's only a question I want to ask. Do you think I could talk to your father or your mother for a moment?'

'You can, to be sure,' the girl replied in a flutter of curiosity. 'Come in, can't you? We're all in the front room.'

Ned, nerving himself for an ordeal, went in. It was a tiny front room with a fire burning in a tiled fireplace. There was a mahogany table at which a boy of twelve seemed to be doing his lessons. Round the fire sat an older girl, a small woman, and a tubby little man with a greying moustache. Ned smiled, and his tone became even more jocular.

'I hope you'll forgive my making a nuisance of myself,' he said. 'My name is Callanan. I live at St Luke's. I wonder if you've ever met my son, Jimmy?'

'Jimmy?' the mother echoed, her hand to her cheek. 'I don't know that I did.'

'I know him,' said the girl who had let him in, in a voice that squeaked with pride.

'Fine!' Ned said. 'At least, you know what I'm talking about. I wonder if you saw him this evening?'

'Jimmy?' the girl replied, taking fright. 'No. Sure, I hardly know him only to salute him. Why? Is anything wrong?'

'Nothing serious, at any rate,' said Ned with a comforting smile. 'It's just that he said he spent the evening here with you. I dare say that's an excuse for being somewhere he shouldn't have been.'

'Well, well, well!' Mrs Ryan said anxiously, joining her hands. 'Imagine saying he was here! Wisha, Mr Callanan, aren't they a caution?'

'A caution against what, though?' Ned asked cheerfully. 'That's what I'd like to know. I'm only sorry he wasn't telling the truth. I'm afraid he wasn't in such charming company. Goodnight, everybody, and thank you.'

'Goodnight, Mr Callanan,' said Mrs Ryan, laying a hand gently on his sleeve. 'And don't be too hard on him! Sure, we were wild ourselves once.'

'Once?' he exclaimed with a laugh. 'I hope we still are. We're not dead yet, Mrs Ryan.'

The same girl showed him out. She had recovered from her fright and looked as though she would almost have liked him to stay.

'Goodnight, Mr Callanan,' she called blithely from the door, and when he turned, she was silhouetted against the lighted doorway, bent halfway over, and waving. He waved back, touched by this glimpse of an interior not so unlike his own, but seen from outside, in all its innocence. It was a shock to emerge on the roadway and see Jimmy still standing where he had left him, though he no longer looked crucified. Instead, with his head down and his hands by his sides, he looked terribly weary. They walked in silence for a few minutes, till they saw the valley of the city and the lamps cascading down the hillsides and breaking below into a foaming lake of light.

'Well,' Ned said gloomily, 'the Ryans seem to be under the impression that you weren't there tonight.'

'I know,' Jimmy replied, as though this were all that might be expected from him.

Something in his tone startled Ned. It no longer seemed to breathe defiance. Instead, it hinted at something very like despair. But why, he thought in exasperation. Why the blazes did he tell me all those lies? Why didn't he tell me even outside the door? Damn it, I gave him every chance.

'Don't you think this is a nice place to live, Dad?' asked Jimmy.

'Is it?' Ned asked sternly.

'Ah, well, the air is better,' said Jimmy with a sigh. They said no more till they reached home.

'Now, go to bed,' Ned said in the hallway. 'I'll consider what to do with you tomorrow.'

Which, as he well knew, was bluff, because he had already decided to do nothing to Jimmy. Somehow he felt that, whatever the boy had done to himself, punishment would be merely an anticlimax, and perhaps a relief. Punishment, he thought, might be exactly what Jimmy would have welcomed at that moment. He went into the sitting-room and poured himself a drink, feeling that if anyone deserved it, he did. He had a curious impression of having been involved in some sort of struggle and escaped some danger to which he could not even give a name.

When he went upstairs, Celia was in bed with a book, and looked up at him with a wide-eyed stare. She proved to be no help to him. 'Jimmy usen't to be like that,' she said wistfully, and he knew she had been lying there regretting the little boy who had come to her with all his troubles.

'But why, why, why, in God's name, did he tell me all those lies?' Ned asked angrily.

'Oh, why do people ever tell lies?' she asked with a shrug.

'Because they hope they won't be found out,' Ned replied. 'Don't you see that's what's so queer about it?'

She didn't, and for hours Ned lay awake, turning it over and over in his mind. It was easy enough to see it as the story of a common falsehood persisted in through some mood of bravado, and each time he thought of it that way he grew angry again. Then, all at once, he would remember the face of Jimmy against the pillar in the moonlight, as though he were being crucified, and give a frustrated sigh.

'Go to sleep!' Celia said once, giving him a vicious nudge.

'I can't, damn it, I can't,' he said, and began all over again.

Why had the kid chosen Ryans' as an excuse? Was that merely to put him further astray, or did it really represent some dream of happiness and fulfilment? The latter explanation he rejected as too simple and sentimental, yet he knew quite well that Ryan's house *had* meant something to the boy, even if it was only an alternative to whatever house he had been in and the company he had met there. Ned could remember himself at that age, and how, when he had abandoned himself to something or somebody, an alternative image would appear. The image that had flashed up in Jimmy's mind, the image that was not one of Hogan's house, was Ryans'. But it needed more than that to explain his own feeling of danger. It was as though Jimmy had deliberately challenged him, if he were the man he appeared to be, to struggle with the demon of fantasy in him and destroy it. It was as though not he but Jimmy had been forcing the pace. At the same time, he realized that this was something he would never know. All he ever would know was that somewhere behind it all were despair and loneliness and terror, under the magic of an autumn night. And yet there were sentimental fools who told you that they would wish to be young again.

Next morning at breakfast, he was cold and aloof, more from embarrassment than hostility. Jimmy, on the other hand, seemed to be in the highest spirits, helping Celia with the breakfast things, saying, 'Excuse me, Daddy,' as he changed Ned's plate. He pushed the sugar bowl towards Ned and said with a grin, 'Daddy likes sugar.'

Ned just restrained himself from flinging the bowl at him. 'As a matter of fact, I do,' he said coldly.

He had done the same sort of thing too often himself. He knew that, with the threat of punishment over his head, Jimmy was scared, as well he might be. It is one thing to be defiant at eleven o'clock at night, another thing altogether to be defiant at eight in the morning.

All day, at intervals, he found himself brooding over it. At lunch he talked to his chief clerk about it, but MacIntyre couldn't advise him. 'God, Ned,' he said impatiently, 'every kid is different. There's no laying down rules. My one told the nuns that her mother was a religious maniac and kicked the statue of the Blessed Virgin around the floor. For God's sake, Ned, imagine Kate kicking a statue around the floor!'

'Difficult, isn't it?' replied Ned with a grin, though to himself he thought complacently that that sort of fantasy was what he would expect from Kate's daughter. Parents so rarely sympathize with one another.

That evening, when he came in, Celia said coolly, 'I don't know what you said to Jimmy, but it seems to have worked.'

Relief came over Ned like a cold shower. He longed to be able to say something calm like 'Oh, good!' or 'Glad I could help' or 'Any time I can advise you again, just let me know'. But he was too honest. He shook his head, still the schoolboy that Celia had loved such a long time ago, and his forehead wrinkled up.

'That's the awful part of it,' he said. 'I said nothing at all to him. For the first time in my life I didn't know what to say. What the hell could I say?'

'Oh, no doubt you said something and didn't notice it,' Celia said confidently. 'There's no such thing in business as an out-and-out free gift.'

(1957)

PUBLIC OPINION

Now I know what you're thinking. You're thinking how nice 'twould be to live in a little town. You could have a king's life in a house like this, with a fine garden and a car so that you could slip up to town whenever you felt in need of company. Living in Dublin, next door to the mail boat and writing things for the American papers, you imagine you could live here and write whatever you liked about Mac-Dunphy of the County Council. Mind, I'm not saying you couldn't say a hell of a lot about him! I said a few things myself from time to time. All I mean is that you wouldn't say it for long. This town broke better men. It broke me and, believe me, I'm no chicken.

When I came here first, ten years ago, I felt exactly the way you do, the way everybody does. At that time, and the same is nearly true today, there wasn't a professional man in this town with a housekeeper under sixty, for fear of what people might say about them. In fact, you might still notice that there isn't one of them who is what you might call 'happily' married. They went at it in too much of a hurry.

Oh, of course, I wasn't going to make that mistake! When I went to choose a housekeeper I chose a girl called Bridie Casey, a handsome little girl of seventeen from a village up the coast. At the same time I took my precautions. I drove out there one day when she was at home, and I had a look at the cottage and a talk with her mother and a cup of tea, and after that I didn't need anyone to recommend her. I knew that anything Bridie fell short in, her mother would not be long in correcting. After that, there was only one inquiry I wanted to make.

'Have you a boy, Bridie?' said I.

'No, Doctor, I have not,' said she with an innocent air that didn't take me in a bit. As a doctor you soon get used to innocent airs.

'Well, you'd better hurry up and get one,' said I, 'or I'm not going to keep you.'

With that she laughed as if she thought I was only joking. I was not joking at all. A housekeeper or maid without a fellow of her own is as bad as a hen with an egg.

'It's no laughing matter,' I said. 'And when you do get a fellow, if you haven't one already, you can tell him I said he could make free with my beer, but if ever I catch you diluting my whiskey I'll sack you on the spot.'

Mind, I made no mistake in Bridie or her mother either. She mightn't be any good in the Shelbourne Hotel, but what that girl could cook she cooked well, and anything she cleaned looked as if it was clean. What's more, she could size a patient up better than I could myself. Make no mistake about it, as housekeepers or maids Irish girls are usually not worth a damn, but a girl from a good Irish home can turn her hand to anything. Of course, she was so good-looking that people who came to the house used to pass remarks about us, but that was only jealousy. They hadn't the nerve to employ a good-looking girl themselves for fear of what people would say. But I knew that as long as a girl had a man of her own to look after she'd be no bother to me.

No, what broke up my happy home was something different altogether. You mightn't understand it, but in a place like this 'tis the devil entirely to get ready money out of them. They'll give you anything else in the world only money. Here, everything is what they call 'friendship'. I suppose the shops give them the habit because a regular customer is always supposed to be in debt and if ever the debt is paid off it's war to the knife. Of course they think a solicitor or a doctor should live the same way, and instead of money what you get is presents: poultry, butter, eggs and meat that a large family could not eat, let alone a single man. Friendship is all very well, but between you and me it's a poor thing for a man to be relying on at the beginning of his career.

I had one patient in particular called Willie Joe Corcoran of Clashanaddig – I buried him last year, poor man, and my mind is easier already – and Willie Joe seemed to think I was always on the verge of starvation. One Sunday I got in from twelve-o'clock Mass and went to the whiskey cupboard to get myself a drink when I noticed the most extraordinary smell. Doctors are sensitive to smells, of course – we have to be – and I shouldn't rest easy till I located that one. I searched the room and I searched the hall and I even poked my head upstairs into the bedrooms before I tried the kitchen. Knowing Bridie, I never even associated the smell with her. When I went in, there she was in a clean white uniform, cooking the dinner, and she looked round at me.

'What the hell is that smell, Bridie?' said I.

She folded her arms and leaned against the wall, as good-looking a little girl as you'd find in five counties.

'I told you before,' says she in her thin, high voice, ' 'tis that side of beef Willie Joe Corcoran left on Thursday. It have the whole house ruined on me.'

'But didn't I tell you to throw that out?' I said.

'You did,' says she, as if I was the most unreasonable man in the world, 'but you didn't tell me where I was going to throw it.'

'What's wrong with the ash can?' said I.

'What's wrong with the ash can?' says she. 'There's nothing wrong with it. Only the ashmen won't be here till Tuesday.'

'Then for God's sake girl, can't you throw it over the wall into the field?'

'Into the field,' says she, pitching her voice up an octave till she sounded like a sparrow in decline. 'And what would people say?'

'Begor, I don't know, Bridie,' I said, humouring her. 'What do *you* think they'd say?'

'They're bad enough to say anything,' says she.

I declare to God I had to look at her to see was she serious. There she was, a girl of seventeen with the face of a nun, suggesting things that I could barely imagine.

'Why, Bridie?' I said, treating it as a joke. 'You don't think they'd say I was bringing corpses home from the hospital to cut up?'

'They said worse,' she said in a squeak, and I saw that she took a very poor view of my powers of imagination. Because you write books, you think you know a few things, but you should listen to the conversation of pious girls in this town.

'About me, Bridie?' said I in astonishment.

'About you and others,' said she. And then, by cripes, I lost my temper with her.

'And is it any wonder they would,' said I, 'with bloody fools like you paying attention to them?'

I have a very wicked temper when I'm roused, and for the time being it scared her more than what people might say of her.

'I'll get Kenefick's boy in the morning and let him take it away,' said she. 'Will I give him a shilling?'

'Put it in the poor box,' said I in a rage. 'I'll be going out to Dr MacMahon's for supper and I'll take it away myself. Any damage that's going to be done to anyone's character can be done to mine. It should be able to stand it. And let me tell you, Bridie Casey, if I was the sort to mind what anyone said about me, you wouldn't be where you are this minute.'

I was very vicious to her, but of course I was mad. After all, I had to take my drink and eat my dinner with that smell round the house, and Bridie in a panic, hopping about me like a hen with hydrophobia. When I went out to the pantry to get the side of beef, she gave a yelp as if I'd trodden on her foot. 'Mother of God!' says she. 'Your new suit!' 'Never mind my new suit,' said I, and I wrapped the beef in a couple of newspapers and heaved it into the back of the car. I declare, it wasn't wishing to me. I had all the windows open, but even then the smell was high, and I went through the town like a coursing match with the people on the footpaths lifting their heads like beagles to sniff after me.

I wouldn't have minded that so much only that Sunday is the one day I have. In those days before I was married I nearly always drove out to Jerry MacMahon's for supper and a game of cards. I knew poor Jerry looked forward to it because the wife was very severe with him in the matter of liquor.

I stopped the car on top of the cliffs to throw out the meat, and just as I was looking for a clear drop I saw a long galoot of a countryman coming up the road towards me. He had a long, melancholy sort of face and mad eyes. Whatever it was about his appearance, I didn't want him to see what I was up to. You might think it funny in a professional man, but that is the way I am.

'Nice evening,' says he.

'Grand evening, thank God,' says I, and not to give him an excuse for being too curious I said: 'That's a powerful view.'

'Well,' says he sourly, just giving it a glance, 'the view is all right but 'tis no good to the people that has to live in it. There is no earning in that view,' says he, and then he cocked his head and began to size me up, and I knew I'd made a great mistake, opening my mouth to him at all. 'I suppose now you'd be an artist?' says he.

You might notice about me that I'm very sensitive to inquisitiveness. It is a thing I cannot stand. Even to sign my name to a telegram is a thing I never like to do, and I hate a direct question.

'How did you guess?' said I.

'And I suppose,' said he, turning to inspect the view again, 'if you painted that, you'd find people to buy it?'

'That's what I was hoping,' said I.

So he turned to the scenery again, and this time he gave it a studied appraisal as if it was a cow at a fair.

'I dare say for a large view like that you'd get nearly five pounds?' said he.

'You would and more,' said I.

'Ten?' said he with his eyes beginning to pop.

'More,' said I.

'That beats all,' he said, shaking his head in resignation. 'Sure, the whole thing isn't worth that. No wonder the country is the way it is. Good luck!'

'Good luck,' said I, and I watched him disappear among the rocks over the road. I waited, and then I saw him peering out at me from behind a rock like some wild mountain animal, and I knew if I stayed there till nightfall I wouldn't shake him off. He was beside himself at the thought of a picture that would be worth as much as a cow, and he probably thought if he stayed long enough he might learn the knack and paint the equivalent of a whole herd of them. The man's mind didn't rise above cows. And, whatever the devil ailed me, I could not give him the satisfaction of seeing what I was really up to. You might think it shortsighted of me, but that is the sort I am.

I got into the car and away with me down to Barney Phelan's pub on the edge of the bay. Barney's pub is the best in this part of the world and Barney himself is a bit of a character; a tall excitable man with wild blue eyes and a holy terror to gossip. He kept filling my glass as fast as I could lower it, and three or four times it was on the tip of my tongue to tell him what I was doing; but I knew he'd make a story out of it for the boys that night and sooner or later it would get back to Willie Joe Corcoran. Bad as Willie Joe was, I would not like to hurt his feelings. That is another

great weakness of mine. I never like hurting people's feelings.

Of course that was a mistake, for when I walked out of
the pub, the first thing I saw was the cliff dweller and two
other yokels peering in at the parcel in the back of my car.
At that I really began to feel like murder. I cannot stand that
sort of unmannerly inquisitiveness.

'Well,' I said, giving the cliff dweller a shoulder out of my
way, 'I hope ye saw something good.'

At that moment Barney came out, drying his hands
in his apron and showing his two front teeth like a
weasel.

'Are them fellows at your car, Doctor?' says he.

'Oho!' said the cliff dweller to his two friends. 'So a doc-
thor is what he is now!'

'And what the hell else did you think he was, you fool?'
asked Barney.

'A painter is what he was when last we heard of him,' said
the lunatic.

'And I suppose he was looking for a little job painting the
huts ye have up in Beensheen?' asked Barney with a sneer.

'The huts may be humble but the men are true,' said the
lunatic solemnly.

'Blast you, man,' said Barney, squaring up to him, 'are you
saying I don't know the doctor since he was in short
trousers?'

'No man knows the soul of another,' said the cliff dweller,
shaking his head again.

'For God's sake, Barney, don't be bothering yourself with
that misfortunate clown,' said I. ' 'Tis my own fault for
bringing the likes of him into the world. Of all the useless
occupations, that and breaking stones are the worst.'

'I would not be talking against breaking stones,' said the
cliff dweller sourly. 'It might not be long till certain people
here would be doing the same.'

At that I let a holy oath out of me and drove off in the

direction of Jerry MacMahon's. When I glanced in the driving mirror I saw Barney standing in the middle of the road with the three yokels around him, waving their hands. It struck me that in spite of my precautions Barney would have a story for the boys that night, and it would not be about Willie Joe. It would be about me. It also struck me that I was behaving in a very uncalled-for way. If I'd been a real murderer trying to get rid of a real corpse I could hardly have behaved more suspiciously. And why? Because I did not want people discussing my business. I don't know what it is about Irish people that makes them afraid of having their business discussed. It is not that it is any worse than other people's business, only we behave as if it was.

I stopped the car at a nice convenient spot by the edge of the bay miles from anywhere. I could have got rid of the beef there and then, but something seemed to have broken in me. I walked up and down that road slowly, looking to right and left to make sure no one was watching. Even then I was perfectly safe, but I saw a farmer crossing a field a mile away up the hill and I decided to wait till he was out of sight. That was where the ferryboat left me, because, of course, the moment he glanced over his shoulder and saw a strange man with a car stopped on the road he stopped himself with his head cocked like an old setter. Mind, I'm not blaming him! I blame nobody but myself. Up to that day I had never felt a stime of sympathy with my neurotic patients, giving themselves diseases they hadn't got, but there was I, a doctor, giving myself a disease I hadn't got and with no excuse whatever.

By this time the smell was so bad I knew I wouldn't get it out of the upholstery for days. And there was Jerry MacMahon up in Cahirnamona, waiting for me with a bottle of whiskey his wife wouldn't let him touch till I got there, and I couldn't go for fear of the way he'd laugh at me. I looked again and saw that the man who'd been crossing the field had changed his mind. Instead he'd come down to the gate and was leaning over it, lighting his pipe while he admired the view of the bay and the mountains.

That was the last straw. I knew now that even if I got rid of the beef my Sunday would still be ruined. I got in the car and drove straight home. Then I went to the whiskey cupboard and poured myself a drink that seemed to be reasonably proportionate to the extent of my suffering. Just as I sat down to it Bridie walked in without knocking. This is one fault I should have told you about – all the time she was with me I never trained her to knock. I declare to God when I saw her standing in the doorway I jumped. I'd always been very careful of myself and jumping was a new thing to me.

'Did I tell you to knock before you came into a room?' I shouted.

'I forgot,' she said, letting on not to notice the state I was in. 'You didn't go to Dr MacMahon's so?'

'I did not,' I said.

'And did you throw away the beef?'

'I didn't,' I said. Then as I saw her waiting for an explanation I added: 'There were too many people around.'

'Look at that now!' she said complacently. 'I suppose we'll have to bury it in the garden after dark?'

'I suppose so,' I said, not realizing how I had handed myself over to the woman, body and bones, holus-bolus.

That evening I took a spade and dug a deep hole in the garden and Bridie heaved in the side of beef. The remarkable thing is that the whole time we were doing it we talked in whispers and glanced up at the backs of other houses in the road to see if we were being watched. But the weight off my mind when it was over! I even felt benevolent to Bridie. Then I went over to Jim Donoghue, the dentist's, and told him the whole story over a couple of drinks. We were splitting our sides over it.

When I say we were splitting our sides I do not mean that this is a funny story. It was very far from being funny for me before it was over. You wouldn't believe the scandal there was about Bridie and myself after that. You'd wonder how people could imagine such things, let alone repeat them. That day changed my whole life . . . Oh, laugh! laugh! I was laughing out the other side of my mouth before it was through. Up to that I'd never given a rap what anyone thought of me, but from that day forth I was afraid of my own shadow. With all the talk there was about us I even had to get rid of Bridie and, of course, inside of twelve months I was married like the rest of them . . . By the way, when I mentioned unhappy marriages I wasn't speaking of my own. Mrs Ryan and myself get on quite well. I only mentioned it to show what might be in store for yourself if ever you were foolish enough to come and live here. A town like this can bend iron. And if you doubt my word, that's only because you don't know what they are saying about you.

(1957)

AN ACT OF CHARITY

THE parish priest, Father Maginnis, did not like the second curate, Father Galvin, and Father Fogarty could see why. It was the dislike of the professional for the amateur, no matter how talented, and nobody could have said that Father Galvin had much in the way of talent. Maginnis was a professional to his fingertips. He drove the right car, knew the right people, and could suit his conversation to any company, even that of women. He even varied his accent to make people feel at home. With Deasy, the owner of the garage, he talked about 'the caw', but to Lavin, the garage hand, he said 'the cyarr', smiling benignly at the homeliness of his touch.

Galvin was thin, pale, irritable, and intense. When he should have kept a straight face he made some stupid joke that stopped the conversation dead; and when he laughed in the proper place at someone else's joke, it was with a slight air of vexation, as though he found it hard to put up with people who made him laugh at all. He worried himself over little embarrassments and what people would think of them, till Fogarty asked bluntly, 'What the hell difference does it make what they think?' Then Galvin looked away sadly and said, 'I suppose you're right.' But Fogarty didn't mind his visits so much except when he had asked other curates in for a drink and a game of cards. Then he took a glass of sherry or something equally harmless and twiddled it awkwardly for half an hour as though it were some sort of patent device for keeping his hands occupied. When one of the curates

made a harmless dirty joke, Galvin pretended to be looking
at a picture so that he didn't have to comment. Fogarty, who
loved giving people nicknames, called him Father Mother's
Boy. He called Maginnis the Old Pro, but when that nick-
name got back, as everything a priest says gets back, it did
Fogarty no harm at all. Maginnis was glad he had a curate
with so much sense.

He sometimes asked Fogarty to Sunday dinner, but he
soon gave up on asking Galvin, and again Fogarty sym-
pathized with him. Maginnis was a professional, even to his
dinners. He basted his meat with one sort of wine and his
chicken with another, and he liked a guest who could tell
the difference. He also liked him to drink two large whiskeys
before dinner and to make sensible remarks about the wine;
and when he had exhausted the secrets of his kitchen he sat
back, smoked his cigar, and told funny stories. They were
very good stories, mostly about priests.

'Did I ever tell you the one about Canon Murphy, Father?'
he would bellow, his fat face beaming. 'Ah, that's damn
good. Canon Murphy went on a pilgrimage to Rome, and
when he came back he preached a sermon on it. "So I had a
special audience with His Holiness, dearly beloved breth-
ren, and he asked me, 'Canon Murphy, where are you
now?' 'I'm in Dromod, Your Holiness,' said I. 'What sort of a
parish is it, Canon Murphy?' says he. 'Ah, 'tis a nice, snug
little parish, Your Holiness,' says I. 'Are they a good class of
people?' says he. 'Well, they're not bad, Your Holiness,'
says I. 'Are they good-living people?' says he. 'Well, they're
as good as the next, Your Holiness,' says I. 'Except when
they'd have a drop taken.' 'Tell me, Canon Murphy,' says he,
'do they pay their dues?' And like that, I was nearly struck
dumb. 'There you have me, Your Holiness!' says I. 'There
you have me.' " '

At heart Fogarty thought Maginnis was a bit of a sham
and that most of his stories were fabrications; but he never
made the mistake of underestimating him, and he enjoyed

the feeling Maginnis gave him of belonging to a group, and that of the best kind – well-balanced, humane, and necessary.

At meals in the curates' house, Galvin had a tendency to chatter brightly and aimlessly that irritated Fogarty. He was full of scraps of undigested knowledge, picked up from papers and magazines, about new plays and books that he would never either see or read. Fogarty was a moody young man who preferred either to keep silent or engage in long emotional discussions about local scandals that grew murkier and more romantic the more he described them. About such things he was hopelessly indiscreet. 'And that fellow notoriously killed his own father,' he said once, and Galvin looked at him in distress. 'You mean he really killed him?' he asked – as though Fogarty did not really mean everything at the moment he was saying it – and then, to make things worse, added, 'It's not something I'd care to repeat – not without evidence, I mean.'

'The Romans used eunuchs for civil servants, but we're more enlightened,' Fogarty said once to Maginnis. 'We prefer the natural ones.' Maginnis gave a hearty laugh; it was the sort of remark he liked to repeat. And when Galvin returned after lunching austerely with some maiden ladies and offered half-baked suggestions, Maginnis crushed him, and Fogarty watched with malicious amusement. He knew it was turning into persecution, but he wasn't quite sure which of the two men suffered more.

When he heard the explosion in the middle of the night, he waited for some further noise to interpret it, and then rose and put on the light. The housekeeper was standing outside her bedroom door in a raincoat, her hands joined. She was a widow woman with a history of tragedy behind her, and Fogarty did not like her; for some reason he felt she had the evil eye, and he always addressed her in his most commanding tone.

'What was that, Mary?' he asked.

'I don't know, Father,' she said in a whisper. 'It sounded as if it was in Father Galvin's room.'

Fogarty listened again. There was no sound from Galvin's room, and he knocked and pushed in the door. He closed the door again immediately.

'Get Dr Carmody quick!' he said brusquely.

'What is it, Father?' she asked. 'An accident?'

'Yes, a bad one. And when you're finished, run out and ask Father Maginnis to come in.'

'Oh, that old gun!' she moaned softly. 'I dreaded it. I'll ring Dr Carmody.' She went hastily down the stairs.

Fogarty followed her and went into the living-room to pick up the Sacred Oils from the cupboard where they were kept. 'I don't know, Doctor,' he heard Mary moaning. 'Father Fogarty said it was an accident.' He returned upstairs and lifted the gun from the bed before anointing the dead man. He had just concluded when the door opened and he saw the parish priest come in, wearing a blue flowered dressing-gown.

Maginnis went over to the bed and stared down at the figure on it. Then he looked at Fogarty over his glasses, his face almost expressionless. 'I was afraid of something like this,' he said knowingly. 'I knew he was a bit unstable.'

'You don't think it could be an accident?' Fogarty asked, though he knew the question sounded ridiculous.

'No,' Maginnis said, giving him a downward look through the spectacles. 'Do you?'

'But how could he bring himself to do a thing like that?' Fogarty asked incredulously.

'Oh, who knows?' said Maginnis, almost impatiently. 'With weak characters it's hard to tell. He doesn't seem to have left any message.'

'Not that I can see.'

'I'm sorry 'twas Carmody you sent for.'

'But he was Galvin's doctor.'

'I know, I know, but all the same he's young and a bit

immature. I'd have preferred an older man. Make no mistake about it, Father, we have a problem on our hands,' he added with sudden resolution. 'A very serious problem.'

Fogarty did not need to have the problem spelled out for him. The worst thing a priest could do was to commit suicide, since it seemed to deny everything that gave his vocation meaning – Divine Providence and Mercy, forgiveness, Heaven, Hell. That one of God's anointed could come to such a state of despair was something the Church could not admit. It would give too much scandal. It was simply an unacceptable act.

'That's his car now, I fancy,' Maginnis said.

Carmody came quickly up the stairs with his bag in his hand and his pink pyjamas showing under his tweed jacket. He was a tall, spectacled young man with a long, humorous clown's face, and in ordinary life adopted a manner that went with his face, but Fogarty knew he was both competent and conscientious. He had worked for some years in an English hospital and developed a bluntness of speech that Fogarty found refreshing.

'Christ!' he said as he took in the scene. Then he went over and looked closely at the body. 'Poor Peter!' he added. Then he took the shotgun from the bedside table where Fogarty had put it and examined it. 'I should have kept a closer eye on him,' he said with chagrin. 'There isn't much I can do for him now.'

'On the contrary, Doctor,' Maginnis said. 'There was never a time when you could do more for him.' Then he gave Fogarty a meaningful glance. 'I wonder if you'd mind getting Jack Fitzgerald for me, Father? Talk to himself, and I needn't warn you to be careful what you say.'

'Oh, I'll be careful,' Fogarty said with gloomy determination. There was something in his nature that always responded to the touch of melodrama, and he knew Maginnis wanted to talk to Carmody alone. He telephoned to Fitzgerald, the undertaker, and then went back upstairs to dress. It was clear he wasn't going to get any more sleep that night.

He heard himself called and returned to Galvin's room. This time he really felt the full shock of it: the big bald parish priest in his dressing-gown and the gaunt young doctor with his pyjama top open under the jacket. He could see the two men had been arguing.

'Perhaps you'd talk to Dr Carmody, Father?' Maginnis suggested benignly.

'There's nothing to talk about, Father Fogarty,' Carmody said, adopting the formal title he ignored when they were among friends. 'I can't sign a certificate saying this was a natural death. You know I can't. It's too unprofessional.'

'Professional or not, Dr Carmody, someone will have to do it,' Maginnis said. 'I am the priest of this parish. In a manner of speaking I'm a professional man too, you know. And this unfortunate occurrence is something that doesn't concern only me and you. It has consequences that affect the whole parish.'

'Your profession doesn't require you to sign your name to a lie, Father,' Carmody said angrily. 'That's what you want me to do.'

'Oh, I wouldn't call that a lie, Dr Carmody,' Maginnis said with dignity. 'In considering the nature of a lie we have to take account of its good and bad effects. I can see no possible good effect that might result from a scandal about the death of this poor boy. Not one! In fact, I can see unlimited harm.'

'So can I,' Fogarty burst out. His voice sounded too loud, too confident, even to his own ears.

'I see,' Carmody said sarcastically. 'And you think we should keep on denouncing the Swedes and Danes for their suicide statistics, just because they don't fake them the way we do. Ah, for God's sake, man, I'd never be able to respect myself again.'

Fogarty saw that Maginnis was right. In some ways Carmody was too immature. 'That's all very well, Jim, but Christian charity comes before statistics,' he said appealingly. 'Forget about the damn statistics, can't you? Father Galvin wasn't only a statistic. He was a human being – somebody we both knew. And what about his family?'

'What about his mother?' Maginnis asked with real pathos. 'I gather you have a mother yourself, Dr Carmody?'

'And you expect me to meet Mrs Galvin tomorrow and tell her her son was a suicide and can't be buried in consecrated ground?' Fogarty went on emotionally. 'Would you like us to do that to your mother if it was your case?'

'A doctor has unpleasant things to do as well, Jerry,' said Carmody.

'To tell a mother that her child is dying?' Fogarty asked. 'A priest has to do that too, remember. Not to tell her that her child is damned.'

But the very word that Fogarty knew had impressed Carmody made the parish priest uncomfortable. 'Fortunately, Father, that is in better hands than yours or mine,' he said curtly. And at once his manner changed. It was as though he was a little bit tired of them both. 'Dr Carmody,' he said, 'I think I hear Mr Fitzgerald. You'd better make up your mind quick. If you're not prepared to sign the death certificate, I'll soon find another doctor who will. That is my simple duty, and I'm going to do it. But as an elderly man who knows a little more about this town than you or Father Fogarty here, I'd advise you not to compel me to bring in another doctor. If word got around that I was forced to do such a thing, it might have very serious effects on your career.'

There was no mistaking the threat, and there was something almost admirable about the way it was made. At the same time, it roused the sleeping rebel in Fogarty. Bluff, he thought angrily. Damn bluff! If Carmody walked out on them at that moment, there was very little the parish priest or anyone else could do to him. Of course, any of the other doctors would sign the certificate, but it wouldn't do them any good either. When people really felt the need for a doctor, they didn't necessarily want the doctor the parish priest approved of. But as he looked at Carmody's sullen, resentful face, he realized that Carmody didn't know his own strength in the way that Maginnis knew his. After all, what had he behind him but a few years in a London hospital, while behind Maginnis was that whole vast, historic organization that he was rightly so proud of.

'I can't sign a certificate that death was due to natural causes,' Carmody said stubbornly. 'Accident, maybe – I don't know. I wasn't here. I'll agree to accident.'

'Accident?' Maginnis said contemptuously, and this time he did not even trouble to use Carmody's title. It was as though he were stripping him of any little dignity he had. 'Young man, accidents with shotguns do not happen to priests at three o'clock in the morning. Try to talk sense!'

And just as Fogarty realized that the doctor had allowed himself to be crushed, they heard Mary let Fitzgerald in. He came briskly up the stairs. He was a small, spare man, built like a jockey. The parish priest nodded in the direction of the bed and Fitzgerald's brows went up mechanically. He was a man who said little, but he had a face and figure too expressive for his character. It was as though all the opinions he suppressed in life found relief in violent physical movements.

'Naturally, we don't want it talked about, Mr Fitzgerald,' said Maginnis. 'Do you think you could handle it yourself?'

The undertaker's eyes popped again, and he glanced swiftly from Maginnis to Carmody and then to Fogarty. He was a great man for efficiency, though; if you had asked him to supply the corpse as well as the coffin, he might have responded automatically, 'Male or female?'

'Dr Carmody will give the certificate, of course?' he asked shrewdly. He hadn't missed much of what was going on.

'It seems I don't have much choice,' Carmody replied bitterly.

'Oh, purely as an act of charity, of course,' Fitz said hastily. 'We all have to do this sort of thing from time to time. The poor relatives have enough to worry them without inquests and things like that. What was the age, Father Maginnis, do you know?' he added, taking out a notebook. A clever little man, thought Fogarty. He had put it all at once upon a normal, businesslike footing.

'Twenty-eight,' said Maginnis.

'God help us!' Fitz said perfunctorily, and made a note. After that he took out a rule.

'I'd better get ready and go to see the Bishop myself,' Maginnis said. 'We'll need his permission, of course, but I haven't much doubt about that. I know he has the reputation for being on the strict side, but I always found him very considerate. I'll send Nora over to help your housekeeper, Father. In the meantime, maybe you'd be good enough to get in touch with the family.'

'I'll see to that, Father,' Fogarty said. He and Carmody followed Maginnis downstairs. He said goodbye and left, and Fogarty's manner changed abruptly. 'Come in and have a drink, Jim,' he said.

'I'd rather not, Jerry,' Carmody said gloomily.

'Come on! Come on! You need one, man! I need one myself and I can't have it.' He shut the door of the living-room behind him. 'Great God, Jim, you could have suspected it?'

'I suppose I should have,' said Carmody. 'I got hints enough if only I might have understood them.'

'But you couldn't, Jim,' Fogarty said excitedly, taking the whiskey from the big cupboard. 'Nobody could. Do you think I ever expected it, and I lived closer to him than you did.'

The front door opened and they heard the slippers of Nora, Maginnis' housekeeper, in the hall. There was a low mumble of talk outside the door, and then the clank of a bucket as the women went up the stairs. Fitzgerald was coming down at the same time, and Fogarty opened the door a little.

'Well, Jack?'

'Well, Father. I'll do the best I can.'

'You wouldn't join us for a—'

'No, Father. I'll have my hands full for the next couple of hours.'

'Goodnight, Jack. And I'm sorry for the disturbance.'

'Ah, 'twas none of your doing. Goodnight, Father.'

The doctor finished his whiskey in a gulp, and his long, battered face had a bitter smile. 'And so this is how it's done!' he said.

'This is how it's done, Jim, and believe me, it's the best way for everybody in the long run,' Fogarty replied with real gravity.

But, looking at Carmody's face, he knew the doctor did not believe it, and he wondered then if he really believed it himself.

When the doctor had gone, Fogarty got on the telephone to a provincial town fifty miles away. The exchange was closed down, so he had to give his message to the police. In ten minutes or so a guard would set out along the sleeping streets to the house where the Galvins lived. That was one responsibility he was glad to evade.

While he was speaking, he heard the parish priest's car set off and knew he was on his way to the Bishop's palace. Then he shaved, and, about eight, Fitzgerald drove up with the coffin in his van. Silently they carried it between them up the stairs. The body was lying decently composed with a simple bandage about the head. Between them they lifted it into the coffin. Fitzgerald looked questioningly at Fogarty and went on his knees. As he said the brief prayer, Fogarty found his voice unsteady and his eyes full of tears. Fitzgerald gave him a pitying look and then rose and dusted his knees.

'All the same there'll be talk, Father,' he said.

'Maybe not as much as there should be, Jack,' Fogarty said moodily.

'We'll take him to the chapel, of course?' Fizgerald went on.

'Everything in order, Jack. Father Maginnis is gone to see the Bishop.'

'He couldn't trust the telephone, of course,' Fitzgerald said, stroking his unshaven chin. 'No fear the Bishop will interfere, though. Father Maginnis is a smart man. You saw him?'

'I saw him.'

'No nerves, no hysterics. I saw other people in the same situation. "Oh, Mr Fitzgerald, what am I going to do?" His mind on essential things the whole time. He's an object lesson to us all, Father.'

'You're right, Jack, he is,' Fogarty said despondently.

Suddenly the undertaker's hand shot out and caught him by the upper arm. 'Forget about it, boy! Forget about it! What else can you do? Why the hell should you break your heart over it?'

Fogarty still had to meet the family. Later that morning, they drove up to the curates' house. The mother was an actressy type and wept a good deal. She wanted somebody to give her a last message, which Fogarty couldn't think up. The sister, a pretty, intense girl, wept a little too, but quietly with her back turned, while the brother, a young man with a great resemblance to Galvin, said little. Mother and brother accepted without protest the ruling that the coffin was not to be opened, but the sister looked at Fogarty and asked, 'You don't think I could see him? Alone? I wouldn't be afraid.' When he said the doctor had forbidden it, she turned her back again, and he had an impression that there was a closer link between her and Galvin than between the others and him.

That evening they brought the body to lie before the altar of the church, and Maginnis received it and said the prayers. The church was crowded, and Fogarty knew with a strange mixture of rejoicing and mortification that the worst was over. Maginnis' master stroke was the new curate, Rowlands, who had arrived within a couple of hours after his own return. He was a tall, thin, ascetic-looking young man, slow-moving and slow-speaking, and Fogarty knew that all eyes were on him.

Everything went in perfect propriety at the Requiem Mass next morning, and after the funeral Fogarty attended the lunch given by Maginnis to the visiting clergy. He almost laughed out loud when he heard Maginnis ask in a low voice, 'Father Healy, did I ever tell you the story of Canon Murphy and the Pope?' All that would follow would be the mourning card with the picture of Galvin and the Gothic lettering that said, '*Ecce Sacerdos Magnus*'. There was no danger of scandal any longer. Carmody would not talk. Fitzgerald would not talk either. None of the five people involved would. Father Galvin might have spared himself the trouble.

As they returned from the church together, Fogarty tried to talk to the new curate about what had happened, but he soon realized that the whole significance of it had escaped Rowlands, and that Rowlands thought he was only overdramatizing it all. Anybody would think he was overdramatizing it, except Carmody. After his supper he would go to the doctor's house, and they would talk about it. Only

Carmody would really understand what it was they had done between them. No one else would.

What lonely lives we live, he thought unhappily.

(1967)

A GREAT MAN

ONCE when I was visiting a famous London hospital, I met
the matron, Miss Fitzgerald, a small, good-looking woman of
fifty. She was Irish, and we discussed acquaintances in
common until I mentioned Dermot O'Malley, and then I
realized that somehow or other I had said the wrong thing.
The matron frowned and went away. A few minutes later
she returned, smiling, and asked me to lunch, in a way that,
for some reason, reminded me of a girl asking a young
fellow for the first time to her home. 'You know, Dr
O'Malley was a great friend of my father,' she said abruptly
and then frowned again.

'Begor, I was,' said O'Malley when I reported this to him
later. 'And I'll tell you a story about it, what's more.'
O'Malley is tall and gentle, and has a wife who is a pain in
the neck, though he treats her with a consideration that I can
only describe as angelic. 'It was when I was a young doctor
in Dublin, and my old professor, Dwyer, advised me to
apply for a job in the hospital in Dooras. Now, you never
heard of Dooras, but we all knew about it then, because that
was in the days of Margaret's father, old Jim Fitzgerald, and
he was known, all right.

'I met him a couple of nights later in a hotel in Kildare
Street. He had come up to Dublin to attend a meeting of
doctors. He was a man with piercing eyes and a long, hard
face – more the face of a soldier than a doctor. The funny
thing was his voice, which was rather high and piping and
didn't seem to go at all with his manner.

' "Dooras is no place for a young man who likes entertain-
ment," he said.

' "Ah, I'm a country boy myself," said I, "so that wouldn't
worry me. And of course, I know the hospital has a great
reputation."

' "So I understand," he said grimly. "You see, O'Malley, I
don't believe in all this centralization that's going on. I know
it's all for the sake of equipment, and equipment is a good
thing, too, but it's taking medicine away from where it
belongs. One of these days, when their centralization breaks
down, they'll find they haven't hospitals, doctors, or anything else."

'By the time I'd left him, I'd as good as accepted the job,
and it wasn't the job that interested me so much as the man.
It could be that, my own father having been a bit of a
waster, I'm attracted to men of strong character, and Fitzgerald was a fanatic. I liked that about him.

'Now, Dwyer had warned me that I'd find Dooras queer,
and Dwyer knew that Dublin hospitals weren't up to much,
but Dooras was dotty. It was an old hospital for infectious
diseases that must have dated from about the time of the
Famine, and Fitzgerald had got a small local committee to
take it over. The first couple of days in it gave me the
horrors, and it was weeks before I even began to see what
Fitzgerald meant by it all. Then I did begin to see that in spite
of all the drawbacks, it worked in a way bigger hospitals
didn't work, and it was happy in a way that bigger hospitals
are never happy. Everybody knew everybody else, and
everybody was madly curious about everybody else, and if
anybody ever gave a party, it wasn't something devised by
the staff to entertain the patients; it was more likely to be
the patients entertaining the staff.

'Partly this was because Margaret Fitzgerald, the woman
you met in London, was the head nurse. I don't know what
she's like now, and from all I can hear she's a bit of a Tartar,
but in those days she was a pretty little thing with an air of

being more efficient than anybody ever was. Whenever you spoke to Margaret, she practically sprang to attention and clicked her heels, and if you were misguided enough to ask her for anything she hadn't handy, she gave you a demonstration of greyhound racing. And, of course, as you can see from the job she has now, she was a damn great nurse.

'But mainly the place worked because of Fitzgerald and his colleagues, the local doctors. Apart from him, none of them struck me as very brilliant, though he himself had a real respect for an old doctor called Pat Duane, a small, round, red-faced man with an old-fashioned choker collar and a wonderful soupy bedside manner. Pat looked as though some kind soul had left him to mature in a sherry cask till all the crude alcohol was drawn out of him. But they were all conscientious; they all listened to advice, even from me – and God knows I hadn't much to offer – and they all deferred in the most extraordinary way to Fitzgerald. Dwyer had described him to me as a remarkable man, and I was beginning to understand the full force of that, because I knew Irish small towns the way only a country boy knows them, and if those men weren't at one another's throats, fighting for every five-bob fee that could be picked up, it was due to his influence. I asked a doctor called MacCarthy about it one night he invited me in for a drink. MacCarthy was a tall old poseur with a terrible passion for local history.

' "Has it occurred to you that Fitzgerald may have given us back our self-respect, young man?" he asked in his pompous way.

' "Your what?" I asked in genuine surprise. In those days it hadn't once occurred to me that a man could at the same time be a show-box and be lacking in self-respect.

' "Oh, come, O'Malley, come!" he said, sounding like the last Duke of Dooras. "As a medical man you are more observant than you pretend. I presume you have met Dr Duane?"

' "I have. Yes," said I.

' "And it didn't occur to you that Dr Duane was ever a victim of alcohol?" he went on portentously. "You understand, of course, that I am not criticizing him. It isn't easy for the professional man in Ireland to maintain his standards of behaviour. Fitzgerald has a considerable respect for Dr Duane's judgement – quite justified, I may add, quite justified. But at any rate, in a very short time Pat eased off on the drink, and even began to read the medical journals again. Now Fitzgerald has him in the hollow of his hand. We all like to feel we are of some use to humanity – even the poor general practitioner . . . But you saw it all for yourself, of course. You are merely trying to pump a poor country doctor."

'Fitzgerald was not pretentious. He liked me to drop in on him when I had an hour to spare, and I went to his house every week for dinner. He lived in an old, uncomfortable family house a couple of miles out on the bay. Normally he was cold, concentrated, and irritable, but when he had a few drinks in he got melancholy, and this for some reason caused him to be indiscreet and say dirty things about his committee and even about the other doctors. "The most interesting thing about MacCarthy," he said to me once, "is that he's the seventh son of a seventh son, and so he can diagnose a case without seeing the patient at all. It leaves him a lot of spare time for local history." I suspected he made the same sort of dirty remarks about me, and that secretly the man had no faith in anyone but himself. I told him so, and I think he enjoyed it. Like all shy men he liked to be insulted in a broad masculine way, and one night when I called him a flaming egotist, he grunted like an old dog when you tickle him and said, "Drink makes you very offensive, O'Malley. Have some more!"

'It wasn't so much that he was an egotist (though he was) as that he had a pernickety sense of responsibility, and whenever he hadn't a case to worry over, he could always

find some equivalent of a fatal disease in the hospital – a
porter who was too cheeky or a nurse who made too free
with the men patients – and he took it all personally and on
a very high level of suffering. He would sulk and snap at
Margaret for days over some trifle that didn't matter to
anyone, and finally reduce her to tears. At the same time, I
suppose it was part of the atmosphere of seriousness he had
created about the makeshift hospital, and it kept us all on our
toes. Medicine was his life, and his gossip was shop. Duane
or MacCarthy or some other local doctor would drop in of
an evening to discuss a case – which by some process I never
was able to fathom had become Fitzgerald's case – and over
the drinks he would grow gloomier and gloomier about our
ignorance, till at last, without a word to any of us, he got up
and telephoned some Dublin specialist he knew. It was part
of the man's shyness that he only did it when he was partly
drunk and could pretend that instead of asking a favour he
was conferring one. Several times I watched that scene with
amusement. It was all carefully calculated, because if he
hadn't had enough to drink he lacked the brass and became
apologetic, whereas if he had had one drink too much he
could not describe what it was about the case that really
worried him. Not that he rated a specialist's knowledge any
higher than ours, but it seemed the best he could do, and if
that didn't satisfy him, he ordered the specialist down, even
when it meant footing the bill himself. It was only then I
began to realize the respect that Dublin specialists had for
him, because Dwyer, who was a terrified little man and
hated to leave home for fear of what might happen him in
out-of-the-way places like Cork and Belfast, would only give
out a gentle moan about coming to Dooras. No wonder
Duane and MacCarthy swore by him, even if for so much of
the time they, like myself, thought him a nuisance.

'Margaret was a second edition of himself, though in her
the sense of responsibility conflicted with everything feminine in her till it became a joke. She was small. She was

pretty, with one of those miniature faces that seem to have been reduced until every coarse line has been refined in them. She moved at twice the normal speed and was for ever fussing and bossing and wheedling, till one of the nurses would lose her temper and say, "Ah, Margaret, will you for God's sake give us time to breathe!" That sort of impertinence would make Margaret scowl, shrug, and go off somewhere else, but her sulks never lasted, as her father's did. The feminine side of her wouldn't sustain them.

'I remember one night when all hell broke loose in the wards, as it usually does in any hospital once a month. Half a dozen patients decided to die all together, and I was called out of bed. Margaret and the other nurse on night duty, Joan Henderson, had brewed themselves a pot of tea in the kitchen, and they were scurrying round with a mug or a bit of seedcake in their hands. I was giving an injection to one of my patients, who should have been ready for discharge. In the next bed was a dying old mountainy man who had nothing in particular wrong with him except old age and a broken heart. I suddenly looked up from what I was doing and saw he had come out of coma and was staring at Margaret, who was standing at the other side of the bed from me, nibbling the bit of cake over which she had been interrupted. She started when she saw him staring at the cake, because she knew what her father would say if ever he heard that she was eating in the wards. Then she gave a broad grin and said in a country accent, "Johnny, would 'oo like a bit of seedcake?" and held it to his lips. He hesitated and then began to nibble too, and then his tongue came out and licked round his mouth, and somehow I knew he was saved. "Tay, Johnny," she said mockingly. "Thot's what 'oo wants now, isn't it?" And that morning as I went through the wards, my own patient was dead, but old Johnny was sitting up, ready for another ten years of the world's hardship. That's nursing.

'Margaret lived at such a pitch of nervous energy that

every few weeks she fell ill. "I keep telling that damn girl to take it easy," her father would say with a scowl at me, but any time there was the least indication that Margaret was taking it easy, he started to air his sufferings with the anguish of an elephant. She was a girl with a real sense of service, and at one time had tried to join a nursing order in Africa, but dropped it because of his hatred of all nursing orders. In itself this was funny, because Margaret was a liberal Catholic who, like St Teresa, was "for the Moors, and martyrdom", but never worried her head about human weaknesses and made no more of an illegitimate baby than if she had them herself every Wednesday, while he was an old-fashioned Catholic and full of obscure prejudices. At the same time, he felt that the religious orders were leaving Ireland without nurses – not that he thought so much of nurses!

' "And I suppose nuns can't be nurses?" Margaret would ask with a contemptuous shrug.

' "How can they?" he would say, in his shrillest voice. "The business of religion is with the soul, not the body. My business is with the body. When I'm done with it, the nuns can have it – or anyone else, for that matter."

' "And why not the soul and the body?" Margaret would ask in her pertest tone.

' "Because you can't serve two masters, girl."

' "Pooh!" Margaret would say with another shrug. "You can't serve one Siamese twin, either."

'As often as I went to dinner in that house, there was hardly a meal without an argument. Sometimes it was about no more than the amount of whiskey he drank. Margaret hated drink, and watched every drop he poured in his glass, so that often, just to spite her, he went on to knock himself out. I used to think that she might have known her father was a man who couldn't resist a challenge. She was as censorious as he was, but she had a pertness and awkwardness that a man rarely had, and suddenly, out of the blue, would

come some piece of impertinence that plunged him into
gloom and made her cringe away to her bedroom, ready for
tears. He and I would go into the big front room, over-
looking Dooras Bay, and without a glance at the view he
would splash enormous tasheens of whiskey into our glasses,
just to indicate how little he cared for her, and say in a
shrill, complaining voice, "I ruined that girl, O'Malley. I
know I did. If her mother was alive, she wouldn't talk to me
that way."

'Generally, they gave the impression of two people who
hated one another with a passionate intensity, but I knew
well that he was crazy about her. He always brought her
back something from his trips to Dublin or Cork, and once,
when I was with him, he casually wasted my whole afternoon looking for something nice for her. It never occurred
to him that I might have anything else to do. But he could
also be thoughtful; for once when for a full week he had
been so intolerable that I could scarcely bring myself to
answer him he grinned and said, "I know exactly what you
think of me, O'Malley. You think I'm an old slave driver."

' "Not exactly," I said, giving him tit for tat. "Just an old
whoor!"

'At this, he gave a great guffaw and handed me a silver
cigarette case, which I knew he must have bought for me in
town the previous day, and added sneeringly, "Now, don't
you be going round saying your work is quite unappreci-
ated."

' "Did I really say that?" I asked, still keeping my end up,
even though there was something familiar about the sentiment.

' "Or if you do, say it over the loudspeaker. Remember,
O'Malley, I hear *everything*." And the worst of it was, he
did!

'Then, one night, when my year's engagement was nearly
ended, I went to his house for dinner. That night there was

no quarrelling, and he and I sat on in the front room, drinking and admiring the view. I should have known there was something wrong, because for once he didn't talk shop. He talked about almost everything else, and all the time he was knocking back whiskey in a way I knew I could never keep pace with. When it grew dark, he said with an air of surprise, "O'Malley, I'm a bit tight. I think we'd better go for a stroll and clear our heads."

'We strolled up the avenue of rhododendrons to the gate and turned left up the hill. It was a wild, rocky bit of country, stopped dead by the roadway and then cascading merrily down the little fields to the bay. There was still a coppery light in the sky, and the reflection of a bonfire on one of the islands, like a pendulum, in the water. The road fell again, between demesne walls and ruined gateways where the last of the old gentry lived, and I was touched – partly, I suppose, by all the whiskey, but partly by the place itself.

' "I'll regret this place when I leave it," I said.

' "Oh, no, you won't," he snapped back at me. "This is no place for young people."

' "I fancy it might be a very pleasant memory if you were in the East End of London," said I.

' "It might," said Fitzgerald, "if you were quite sure you wouldn't have to go back to it. That's what worries me about Margaret."

'I had never noticed him worrying very much about Margaret – or anyone else, for that matter – so I took it as merely a matter of form.

' "Margaret seems to do very well in it," I said.

' "It's no place for Margaret," he said sharply. "People need friends of their own age and ideas old men like myself can't supply. It's largely my fault for letting her come back here at all. I made this place too much of my life, and that's all right for a man, but it's not good enough for a high-spirited girl like that."

' "But doesn't Margaret have friends here?" I asked, trying to comfort him.

' "She has friends enough, but not of her own age," he said. "She's too mature for the girls here that are her own age. Not that I ever cared much for her friends from Dublin," he added shortly. "They struck me as a lot of show-boxes. I don't like those intellectual Catholics, talking to me about St Thomas Aquinas. I never read St Thomas Aquinas, and from all I can hear I haven't missed much. But young people have to make their own mistakes. All the men around here seem to want is some good-natured cow who'll agree to everything they say, and because she argues with them they think she's pert and knowing. Well, she *is* pert, and she *is* knowing – I realize that as well as anybody. But there's more than that to her. They'd have said the same about me, only I proved to them that I knew what I was doing."

'Suddenly I began to realize what he was saying, and I was frightened out of my wits. I said to myself that it was impossible, that a man like Fitzgerald could never mean a thing like that, but at the same time I felt that he did mean it, and that it had been in his mind from the first night he met me. I muttered something about her having more chances in Dublin.

' "That's the trouble," he said. "She didn't know what she was letting herself in for when she came back here, and no more did I. Now she won't leave, because I'd be here on my own. Well, I would be on my own, and I know I wouldn't like it, but still I have my work to do, and for a man that's enough. I like pitting my wits against parish priests and county councillors and nuns. Besides, when you reach my age you realize that you could have worse, and they'll let me have my own way for the time I have left me. But I haven't so long to live, and when I die, they'll have some champion footballer running the place, and Margaret will be taking orders from the nuns. She thinks now that she won't mind, but she won't do it for long. I know the girl. She ought to marry, and then she'd have to go wherever her husband took her."

' "But you don't really think the hospital will go to pieces like that?" I asked, pretending to be deeply concerned, but really only trying to head Fitzgerald off the subject he seemed to have on his mind. "I mean, don't you think Duane and MacCarthy will hold it together?"

' "How can they?" he asked querulously. "It's not their life, the way it's been mine. I don't mean they won't do their best, but the place will go to pieces just the same. It's a queer feeling, Dermot, when you realize that nothing in the world outlasts the man that made it."

'That sentence was almost snapped at me, out of the side of his mouth, and yet it sounded like a cry of pain – maybe because he'd used my Christian name for the first time. He was not a man to use Christian names. I didn't know what to say.

' "Of course, I should have had a son to pass on my responsibilities to," he added wonderingly. "I'm not any good with girls. I dare say that was why I liked you, the first time we met – because I might have had a son like you."

'Then I couldn't bear it any longer, and it broke from me. "And it wasn't all on one side!"

' "I guessed that. In certain ways we're not so unlike. And that's what I really wanted to say to you before you go. If ever you and Margaret got to care for one another, it would mean a lot to me. She won't have much, but she'll never be a burden on anybody, and if ever she marries, she'll make a good wife."

'It was the most embarrassing moment of my life – and mind, it wasn't embarrassing just because I was being asked to marry a nice girl I'd never given a thought to. I'm a country boy, and I knew all about "made" matches by the time I was seventeen, and I never had anything but contempt for the snobs that pretend to despise them. Damn good matches the most of them are, and a thousand times better than the sort you see nowadays that seem to be made up out of novelettes or moving pictures! Still and all, it's different when it comes to your own turn. I suppose it's only at a moment like that you realize you're just as silly as any little servant girl. But it wasn't only that. It was because I was being proposed to by a great man, a fellow I'd looked up to in a way I never looked up to my own father, and I couldn't do the little thing he wanted me to do. I muttered some nonsense about never having been able to think about marriage – as if there ever was a young fellow that hadn't thought about it every night of his life! – and he saw how upset I was and squeezed my arm.

' "What did I tell you?" he said. "I knew I was drunk, and if she ever gets to hear what I said to you, she'll cut me in little bits."

'And that tone of his broke my heart. I don't even know if you'll understand what I mean, but all I felt was grief to think a great man who'd brought life to a place where life never was before would have to ask a favour of me, and me not to be able to grant it. Because all the time I wanted to be cool and suave and say of course I'd marry his daughter, just to show the way I felt about himself, and I was too much of a coward to do it. In one way, it seemed so impossible, and in another it seemed such a small thing.

'Of course, we never resumed the conversation, but that didn't make it any easier, because it wasn't only between myself and him; it was between me and Margaret. The moment I had time to think of it, I knew Fitzgerald was too much of a gentleman to have said anything to me without first making sure that she'd have me.

'Well, you know the rest yourself. When he died, things happened exactly the way he'd prophesied; a local foot-baller got his job, and the nuns took over the nursing, and there isn't a Dublin doctor under fifty that could even tell you where Dooras is. Fitzgerald was right. Nothing in the

world outlasts a man. Margaret, of course, has a great reputation, and I'm told on the best authority that there isn't a
doctor in St Dorothy's she hasn't put the fear of God into, so
I suppose it's just as well that she never got the opportunity
to put it into me. Or don't you agree?'

I didn't, of course, as O'Malley well knew. Anyway, he
could hardly have done much worse for himself. And I had
met Margaret, and I had seen her autocratic airs, but they
hadn't disturbed me much. She was just doing it on tempera-
ment, rather than technique – a very Irish way, and probably not so unlike her father's. I knew I didn't have to tell
O'Malley that. He was a gentleman himself, and his only
reason for telling me the story was that already, with the
wisdom that comes of age, he had begun to wonder whether
he had not missed something in missing Margaret Fitzgerald.
I knew that he had.

(1958)

A STORY BY MAUPASSANT

PEOPLE who have not grown up in a provincial town won't know what I mean when I say what Terry Coughlan meant to me. People who have won't need to know.

As kids we lived a few doors from each other on the same terrace, and his sister, Tess, was a friend of my sister, Nan. There was a time when I was rather keen on Tess myself. She was a small, plump, gay little thing, with rosy cheeks like apples, and she played the piano very well. In those days I sang a bit, though I hadn't much of a voice. When I sang Mozart, Beethoven, or even Wagner, Terry would listen with brooding approval. When I sang commonplace stuff, Terry would make a face and walk out. He was a good-looking lad with a big brow and curly black hair, a long, pale face and a pair of intent dark eyes. He was always well spoken and smart in his appearance. There was nothing sloppy about him.

When he could not learn something by night he got up at five in the morning to do it, and whatever he took up he mastered. Even as a boy he was always looking forward to the day when he'd have money enough to travel, and he taught himself French and German in the time it took me to find out I could not learn Irish. He was cross with me for wanting to learn it; according to him it had 'no cultural significance', but he was crosser still with me because I couldn't learn it. 'The first thing you should learn to do is to work,' he would say gloomily. 'What's going to become of you if you don't?' He had read somewhere that when Keats was depressed, he had a wash and brush-up. Keats was his god. Poetry was never much in my line, except Shelley, and Terry didn't think much of him.

We argued about it on our evening walks. Maybe you don't remember the sort of arguments you had when you were young. Lots of people prefer not to remember, but I like thinking of them. A man is never more himself than when he talks nonsense about God, Eternity, prostitution, and the necessity for having mistresses. I argued with Terry that the day of poetry was over, and that the big boys of modern literature were the fiction writers – the ones we'd heard of in Cork at that time, I mean – the Russians and Maupassant.

'The Russians are all right,' he said to me once. 'Maupassant you can forget.'

'But why, Terry?' I asked.

'Because whatever you say about the Russians, they're noble,' he said. 'Noble' was a great word of his at the time: Shakespeare was 'noble', Turgenev was 'noble', Beethoven was 'noble'. 'They are a religious people, like Greeks, or the English of Shakespeare's time. But Maupassant is slick and coarse and commonplace. Are his stories literature?'

'Ah, to hell with literature!' I said. 'It's life.'

'Life in this country?'

'Life in his own country, then.'

'But how do you know?' Terry asked, stopping and staring at me. 'Humanity is the same here as anywhere else. If he's not true of the life we know, he's not true of any sort of life.'

Then he got the job in the monks' school and I got the job in Carmody's and we began to drift apart. There was no quarrel. It was just that I liked company and Terry didn't. I got in with a wild group – Marshall and Redmond and Donnelan, the solicitor – and we sat up until morning, drinking and settling the future of humanity. Terry came with us once, but he didn't talk, and when Donnelan began

to hold forth on Shaw and the Life Force I could see his face
getting dark. You know Donnelan's line – 'But what I mean
– what I want to say – Jasus, will somebody let me talk? I
have something important to say.' We all knew that Donnelan was a bit of a joke, but when I said goodnight to Terry
in the hall he turned on me with an angry look.

'Do those friends of yours do anything but talk?' he
asked.

'Never mind, Terry,' I said. 'The Revolution is coming.'

'Not if they have anything to say to it,' Terry said, and
walked away from me. I stood there for a while, feeling
sorry for myself, as you do when you know that the end of a
friendship is in sight. It didn't make me happier when I went
back to the room and Donnelan looked at me as if he didn't
believe his eyes.

'Magner,' he asked, 'am I dreaming or was there someone
with you?'

Suddenly, for no particular reason, I lost my temper.

'Yes, Donnelan,' I said. 'But somebody I wouldn't expect
you to recognize.'

That, I suppose, was the last flash of the old love, and after
that it was bogged down in argument. Donnelan said that
Terry lacked flexibility – flexibility!

Occasionally I met Tess with her little shopping basket
and her round rosy cheeks, and she would say reproachfully, 'Ah, Ted, aren't you becoming a great stranger? What
did we do to you at all?' And a couple of times I dropped
round to sing a song and borrow a book, and Terry told me
about his work as a teacher. He was a bit disillusioned with
his job, and you wouldn't wonder. Some of the monks kept a
mackintosh and muffler handy so that they could drop out
to the pictures after dark with some doll. And then there
was a thundering row when Terry discovered that a couple
of his brightest boys were being sent up for public examinations under the names of notorious ignoramuses, so
as to bolster up the record. When Brother Dunphy, the

headmaster, argued with Terry that it was only a simple
act of charity, Terry replied sourly that it seemed to him
more like a criminal offence. After that he got the reputation
of being impossible and was not consulted when Patrick
Dempsey, the boy he really liked, was put up for examination as Mike MacNamara, the County Councillor's son –
Mike the Moke, as Terry called him.

Now, Donnelan is a gasbag, and, speaking charitably, a bit
of a fool, but there were certain things he learned in his
Barrack Street slum. One night he said to me, 'Ted, does that
fellow Coughlan drink?' 'Drink?' I said, laughing outright at
him. 'Himself and a sparrow would have about the same
consumption of liquor.' Nothing ever embarrassed Donnelan, who had the hide of a rhinoceros.

'Well, you might be right,' he said reasonably, 'but, begor,
I never saw a sparrow that couldn't hold it.'

I thought myself that Donnelan was dreaming, but next
time I met Tess I sounded her. 'How's that brother of yours
keeping?' I asked. 'Ah, fine, Ted, why?' she asked, as though
she was really surprised. 'Oh, nothing,' I said. 'Somebody
was telling me that he wasn't looking well.'

'Ah, he's that way this long time, Ted,' she replied, 'and
'tis nothing only the want of sleep. He studies too hard at
night, and then he goes wandering all over the country,
trying to work off the excitement. Sure, I'm always at
him!'

That satisfied me. I knew Tess couldn't tell me a lie. But
then, one moonlight night about six months later, three or
four of us were standing outside the hotel – the night porter
had kicked us out in the middle of an argument, and we
were finishing it there. Two was striking from Shandon
when I saw Terry coming up the pavement towards us. I
never knew whether he recognized me or not, but all at once
he crossed the street, and even I could see that the man was
drunk.

'Tell me,' said Donnelan, peering across at him, 'is that a

sparrow I see at this hour of night?' All at once he spun round on his heels, splitting his sides with laughing. 'Magner's sparrow!' he said. 'Magner's sparrow!' I hope in comparing Donnelan with a rhinoceros I haven't done injustice to either party.

I saw then what was happening. Terry was drinking all right, but he was drinking unknown to his mother and sister. You might almost say he was drinking unknown to himself. Other people could be drunkards, but not he. So he sat at home reading, or pretending to read, until late at night, and then slunk off to some low pub on the quays where he hoped people wouldn't recognize him, and came home only when he knew his family was in bed.

For a long time I debated with myself about whether I shouldn't talk to him. If I made up my mind to do it once, I did it twenty times. But when I ran into him in town, striding slowly along, and saw the dark, handsome face with the slightly ironic smile, I lost courage. His mind was as keen as ever – it may even have been a shade too keen. He was becoming slightly irritable and arrogant. The manners were as careful and the voice was as pleasant as ever – a little too much so. The way he raised his hat high in the air to some woman who passed and whipped the big handkerchief from his breast pocket reminded me of an old actor going down in the world. The farther down he went the worse the acting got. He wouldn't join me for a drink; no, he had this job that simply must be finished tonight. How could I say to him, 'Terry, for God's sake, give up trying to pretend you have work to do. I know, you're an impostor and you're drinking yourself to death.' You couldn't talk like that to a man of his kind. People like him are all of a piece; they have to stand or fall by something inside themselves.

He was forty when his mother died, and by that time it looked as though he'd have Tess on his hands for life as well. I went back to the house with him after the funeral. He was cruelly broken up. I discovered that he had spent his first few weeks abroad that summer and he was full of it. He had stayed in Paris and visited the cathedrals round, and they had made a deep impression on him. He had never seen real architecture before. I had a vague hope that it might have jolted him out of the rut he had been getting into, but I was wrong. It was worse he was getting.

Then, a couple of years later I was at home one evening, finishing up some work, when a knock came to the door. I opened it myself and saw old Pa Hourigan, the policeman, outside. Pa had a schoolgirl complexion and a white moustache, china-blue eyes and a sour elderly mouth, like a baby who has learned the facts of life too soon. It surprised me because we never did more than pass the time of day.

'May I speak to you for a moment, Mr Magner?' he asked modestly. ' 'Tis on a rather private matter.'

'You can to be sure, Sergeant,' I said, joking him. 'I'm not a bit afraid. 'Tis years since I played ball on the public street. Have a drink.'

'I never touch it, going on night duty,' he said, coming into the front room. 'I hope you will pardon my calling, but you know I am not a man to interfere in anyone else's private affairs.'

By this time he had me puzzled and a bit anxious. I knew him for an exceptionally retiring man, and he was clearly upset.

'Ah, of course you're not,' I said. 'No one would accuse you of it. Sit down and tell me what the trouble is.'

'Aren't you a friend of Mr Coughlan, the teacher?' he asked.

'I am,' I said.

'Mr Magner,' he said, exploding on me, 'can you do nothing with the man?'

I looked at him for a moment and had a premonition of disaster.

'Is it as bad as that?' I asked.

'It cannot go on, Mr Magner,' he said, shaking his head. 'It cannot go on. I saved him before. Not because he was anything to me, because I hardly knew the man. Not even because of his poor decent sister, though I pity her with my whole heart and soul. It was for the respect I have for education. And you know that, Mr Magner,' he added earnestly, meaning (which was true enough) that I owed it to him that I had never paid a fine for drinking during prohibited hours.

'We all know it, Sergeant,' I said. 'And I assure you, we appreciate it.'

'No one knows, Mr Magner,' he went on, 'what sacrifices Mrs Hourigan and myself made to put that boy of ours through college, and I would not give it to say to him that an educated man could sink so low. But there are others at the barrack who don't think the way I do. I name no names, Mr Magner, but there are those who would be glad to see an educated man humiliated.'

'What is it, Sergeant?' I asked. 'Drink?'

'Mr Magner,' he said indignantly, 'when did I ever interfere with an educated man for drinking? I know when a man has a lot on his mind he cannot always do without stimulants.'

'You don't mean drugs?' I asked. The idea had crossed my mind once or twice.

'No, Mr Magner, I do not,' he said, quivering with indignation. 'I mean those low, loose, abandoned women that I would have whipped and transported.'

If he had told me that Terry had turned into a common thief, I couldn't have been more astonished and horrified. Horrified is the word.

'You don't mind my saying that I find that very hard to believe, Sergeant?' I asked.

'Mr Magner,' he said with great dignity, 'in my calling a man does not use words lightly.'

'I know Terry Coughlan since we were boys together, and

I never as much as heard an unseemly word from him,' I said.

'Then all I can say, Mr Magner, is that I'm glad, very glad that you've never seen him as I have, in a condition I would not compare to the beasts.' There were real tears in the old man's eyes. 'I spoke to him myself about it. At four o'clock this morning I separated him from two of those vile creatures that I knew well were robbing him. I pleaded with him as if he was my own brother. "Mr Coughlan," I said, "what will your soul do at the Judgement?" and Mr Magner, in decent society I would not repeat the disgusting reply he made me.'

'Corruptio optimi pessima,' I said to myself.

'That is Latin, Mr Magner,' the old policeman said with real pleasure.

'And it means "Lilies that fester smell far worse than weeds," Sergeant,' I said. 'I don't know if I can do anything. I suppose I'll have to try. If he goes on like this he'll destroy himself, body and soul.'

'Do what you can for his soul, Mr Magner,' whispered the old man, making for the door. 'As for his body, I wouldn't like to answer.' At the door he turned with a mad stare in his blue eyes. 'I would not like to answer,' he repeated, shaking his grey pate again.

It gave me a nasty turn. Pa Hourigan was happy. He had done his duty but mine still remained to be done. I sat for an hour, thinking about it, and the more I thought the more hopeless it seemed. Then I put on my hat and went out.

Terry lived at that time in a nice little house on College Road; a little red-brick villa with a bow window. He answered the door himself, a slow, brooding, black-haired man with a long pale face. He didn't let on to be either surprised or pleased.

'Come in,' he said with a crooked smile. 'You're a great stranger, aren't you?'

'You're a bit of a stranger yourself, Terry,' I said jokingly. Then Tess came out, drying her hands in her apron. Her little cheeks were as rosy as ever, but the gloss was gone. I had the feeling that now there was nothing much she didn't know about her brother. Even the nervous smile suggested that she knew what I had come for – of course, old Hourigan must have brought him home.

'Ah, Ted, 'tis a cure for sore eyes to see you,' she said. 'You'll have a cup? You will, to be sure.'

'You'll have a drink,' Terry said.

'Do you know, I think I will, Terry,' I said, seeing a nice natural opening for the sort of talk I had in mind.

'Ah, you may as well have both,' said Tess, and a few minutes later she brought in the tea and cake. It was like old times until she left us, and then it wasn't. Terry poured out the whiskey for me and the tea for himself, though his hand was shaking so badly that he could scarcely lift his cup. It was not all pretence; he didn't want to give me an opening, that was all. There was a fine print over his head – I think it was a Constable of Salisbury Cathedral. He talked about the monastery school, the usual clever, bitter, contemptuous stuff about monks, inspectors and pupils. The whole thing was too carefully staged, the lifting of the cup and the wiping of the moustache, but it hypnotized me. There was something there you couldn't do violence to. I finished my drink and got up to go.

'What hurry is on you?' he asked irritably.

I mumbled something about it's getting late.

'Nonsense!' he said. 'You're not a boy any longer.'

Was he just showing off his strength of will or hoping to put off the evil hour when he would go slinking down the quays again?

'Ah, they'll be expecting me,' I said, and then, as I used to do when we were younger, I turned to the bookcase. 'I see you have a lot of Maupassant at last,' I said.

'I bought them last time I was in Paris,' he said, standing

beside me and looking at the books as though he were seeing them for the first time.

'A death-bed repentance?' I asked lightly, but he ignored me.

'I met another great admirer of his there,' he said sourly. 'A lady you should meet some time.'

'I'd love to if I ever get there,' I said.

'Her address is the Rue de Grenelle,' he said, and then with a wild burst of mockery, 'the left-hand pavement.'

At last his guard was down, and it was Maupassant's name that had done it. And still I couldn't say anything. An angry blush mounted his pale dark face and made it sinister in its violence.

'I suppose you didn't know I indulged in that hideous vice?' he snarled.

'I heard something,' I said. 'I'm sorry, Terry.'

The angry flush died out of his face and the old brooding look came back.

'A funny thing about those books,' he said. 'This woman I was speaking about, I thought she was bringing me to a hotel. I suppose I was a bit muddled with drink, but after dark one of these places is much like another. "This isn't a hotel," I said when we got upstairs. "No," she said, "it's my room." '

As he told it, I could see that he was living it all over again, something he could tell nobody but myself.

'There was a screen in the corner. I suppose it's the result of reading too much romantic fiction, but I thought there might be somebody hidden behind it. There was. You'd never guess what?'

'No.'

'A baby,' he said, his eyes boring through me. 'A child of maybe eighteen months. I wouldn't know. While I was looking, she changed him. He didn't wake.'

'What was it?' I asked, searching for the message that he obviously thought the incident contained. 'A dodge?'

'No,' he said almost grudgingly. 'A country girl in trouble, trying to support her child, that's all. We went to bed and she fell asleep. I couldn't. It's many years now since I've been able to sleep like that. So I put on the light and began to read one of the books that I carried round in my pocket. The light woke her and she wanted to see what I had. "Oh, Maupassant," she said. "He's a great writer." "Is he?" I said. I thought she might be repeating something she'd picked up from one of her customers. She wasn't. She began to talk about *Boule de Suif*. It reminded me of the arguments we used to have in our young days.' Suddenly he gave me a curious boyish smile. 'You remember, when we used to walk up the river together.'

'Oh, I remember,' I said with a sigh.

'We were terrible young idiots, the pair of us,' he said sadly. 'Then she began to talk about *The Tellier Household*. I said it had poetry. "Oh, if it's poetry you want, you don't go to Maupassant. You go to Vigny, you go to Musset, but Maupassant is life, and life isn't poetry. It's only when you see what life can do to you that you realize what a great writer Maupassant is." ... Wasn't that an extraordinary thing to happen?' he asked fiercely, and again the angry colour mounted his cheeks.

'Extraordinary,' I said, wondering if Terry himself knew how extraordinary it was. But it was exactly as if he were reading the thoughts as they crossed my mind.

'A prostitute from some French village, a drunken old waster from an Irish provincial town, lying awake in the dawn in Paris, discussing Maupassant. And the baby, of course. Maupassant would have made a lot of the baby.'

'I declare to God, I think if I'd been in your shoes, I'd have brought them back with me,' I said. I knew when I said it that I was talking nonsense, but it was a sort of release for all the bitterness inside me.

'What?' he asked, mocking me. 'A prostitute and her

baby? My dear Mr Magner, you're becoming positively romantic in your old age.'

'A man like you should have a wife and children,' I
said.

'Ah, but that's a different story,' he said malevolently.
'Maupassant would never have ended a story like that.'

And he looked at me almost triumphantly with those
mad, dark eyes. I knew how Maupassant would have ended
that story all right. Maupassant, as the girl said, was life, and
life was pretty nearly through with Terry Coughlan.

(1945–1968)

LOST FATHERLANDS

ONE spring day, Father Felix in the monastery sent word down to Spike Ward, the motor-driver, to pick up a gentleman for the four-fifteen train. Spike had no notion of who the gentleman was. All sorts came and went to that lonesome monastery up the mountain: people on pilgrimage, drunks going in for a cure, cures coming out for a drunk, men joining the novitiate, and others leaving it, some of them within twenty-four hours – they just took one good look at the place and bolted. One of the novices stole a suit of overalls left behind by a house painter and vanished across the mountain. As Spike often said, if it was him he wouldn't have waited to steal the overalls.

It lay across the mountainside, a gaunt, Victorian barracks. Spike drove up to the guesthouse, which stood away in by the end of the chapel. Father Felix, the Guestmaster, was waiting on the steps with the passenger – a tall, well-built, middle-aged man with greying hair. Father Felix himself inclined to fat; he wore big, shiny glasses, and his beard cascaded over his chest. Spike and the passenger loaded the trunk and bag, and Spike noticed that they were labelled for Canada. The liner was due at Cobh two days later.

'Goodbye now,' Father Felix said, shaking the passenger's hand. 'And mind and don't lead Spike into bad ways on me. He's a fellow I have my eye on this long time. When are you coming up to us for good, Spike?' he asked gravely.

'When ye take a few women into the order, Father,' Spike

replied in his thin drawl. 'What this place needs is a woman's hand.'

The passenger sat in front with Spike, and they chatted as they drove down the hill, glancing back at the monks working in the fields behind the monastery. You should see them from a long way off, like magpies.

'Was it on a holiday you were?' asked Spike, not meaning to be inquisitive, only to make conversation.

'A long holiday,' said the passenger, with a nod and a smile.

'Ah, well, everyone to his taste,' Spike said tolerantly. 'I suppose a lot depends on what you're used to. I prefer a bit of a change myself, like Father Felix's dipsos.'

'He has a few of them up there now,' said the passenger, with a quiet amusement that told Spike he wasn't one of them.

'Well, I'm sure I hope the poor souls are enjoying it,' said Spike with unction.

'They weren't enjoying it much at three this morning,' said the passenger in the same tone. 'One of them was calling for his mother. Father Felix was with him for over an hour, trying to calm him.'

'Not criticizing the good man, 'tisn't the same thing at all,' Spike said joyously.

'Except for the feeding bottle,' said the passenger. And then, as though he were slightly ashamed of his own straight-faced humour: 'He does a wonderful job on them.'

'Well, they seem to have great faith in him,' Spike said, without undue credulity. 'He gets them from England and all parts – a decent little man.'

'And a saintly little man,' the passenger said, almost reproachfully.

'I dare say,' Spike said, without enthusiasm. 'He'd want to be, judging by the specimens I see.'

They reached town with about three-quarters of an hour

to spare, and put the trunk and bag in the stationmaster's office. Old Mick Hurley, the stationmaster, was inside, and looked at the bags over his glasses. Even on a warm day, in his own office, he wore his braided frock-coat and uniform cap.

'This is a gent from the monastery, Mick,' said Spike. 'He's travelling by the four-fifteen. Would he have time for the pictures?'

But Spike might have known the joke would be lost on Mick, who gave a hasty glance at the clock behind him and looked alarmed. 'He'd hardly have time for that,' he said. 'She's only about twenty-five minutes late.'

'You have over an hour to put in,' said Spike as they left the office. 'You don't want to be sitting round there the whole time. Hanagan's lounge is comfortable enough, if you like a drink.'

'Will you have one with me?' asked the passenger.

'I don't know will I have the time,' Spike said. 'I have another call at four. I'll have one drink with you, anyway.'

They went into the bar, which was all done up in chromium, with concealed lighting. Tommy Hanagan, the Yank, was behind the bar himself. He was a tall, fresh-faced, rather handsome man, with fair hair of a dirty colour and smoke-blue eyes. His hat was perched far back on his head. Spike often said Tommy Hanagan was the only man he knew who could make a hat speak. He had earned the price of his public-house working in Boston and, according to him, had never ceased to regret his return. Tommy looked as though he lived in hopes that some day, when he did something as it should be done, it would turn out to be a convenience to somebody. So far, it had earned him nothing but mockery, and sometimes his blue eyes had a slightly bewildered expression, as though he were wondering what he was doing in that place at all.

Spike loved rousing him. All you had to do was give him

one poke about America and the man was off, good for an hour's argument. America was the finest goddam country on the face of the earth, and the people that criticized it didn't know what they were talking about. In America, even the priests were friends: 'Tommy, where the hell am I going to get a hundred dollars?' 'I'll get it for you, Father Joe.' In Ireland, it was '*Mister* Hanagan, don't you consider five pounds is a bit on the small side?' 'And I don't,' the Yank would say, pulling up his shirtsleeves. 'I'd sooner give a hundred dollars to a friend than fifteen to a bastard like that.' The same with the women. Over there, an Irishman would say, 'I'll do the washing up, Mary.' Here it was 'Where's that bloody tea, woman?' And then bawling her out for it! Not, as Spike noticed, that this ever prevented the Yank from bawling out his own wife twenty times a day. And Spike suspected that however he might enjoy rousing the Yank, the Yank enjoyed it more. It probably gave the poor man the illusion of being alive.

'What are you drinking?' the passenger asked in his low voice.

'Whiskey,' said Spike. 'I have to take whiskey every time I go up to that monastery. It's to restore the circulation.'

'Beer for me, please,' said the passenger.

'Your circulation is easily damaged, Spike,' said Hanagan as he turned to the whiskey bottle.

'If you knew as much about that place as I do, you'd be looking for whiskey, too.'

'Who said I don't know about it?' blustered Hanagan. 'I know as much about it as you do; maybe more.'

'You do,' Spike said mockingly. 'Yourself and the kids went up there two years ago, picking primroses. I heard about it. Ye brought the flask and had tea up the mountain two miles away. "Oh, what a lovely place the monks have! Oh, what a wonderful life they have up here!' Damn all you care about the poor unfortunates, getting up at half past one of a winter's morning and waiting till half five for a bit of breakfast.'

The Yank sprawled across the counter, pushing his hat back a shade farther. It was set for reasonable discussion. 'But what's that, only habit?' he asked.

'Habit!'

'What else is it?' the Yank asked appealingly. 'I have to get up at half past six every morning, winter and summer, and I have to worry about a wife and kids, and education and doctors for them, and paying income tax, which is more than the monks have to do.'

'Give me the income tax every time!' said Spike. 'Even the wife!'

'The remarkable thing about this country,' said Hanagan, 'is that they'll only get up in the morning when no one asks them to. I never asked the monks to get up at half past one. All I ask is that the people in this blooming town will get up at half past eight and open their shops by nine o'clock. And how many of them will do it?'

'And what the hell has that to do with the argument?' asked Spike, not that he thought it had anything to do with it. He knew only too well the Yank's capacity for getting carried away on a tide of his own eloquence.

'Well, what after all does the argument boil down to?' retorted Hanagan. 'The argument is that no one in this blooming country is respected for doing what he ought to do – only for doing what no one ever asked him to do.'

'Are people to sit down and wait for someone to ask them to love God?' the passenger growled suddenly. Spike noticed that even though he mentioned God, he looked a nasty customer to cross in a discussion.

'I didn't say that,' Hanagan replied peaceably. 'But do you know this town?'

'No.'

'I do,' said Hanagan. 'I know it since I was a kid. I spent

eighteen years out of it, and for all the difference it made to the town, I might have been out of it for a week. It's dead. The people are dead. They're no use to God or man.'

'You didn't answer my question.'

'You're talking about one sort of responsibility,' said Hanagan. 'I'm only saying there are other responsibilities. Why can't the people here see that they have a responsibility to the unfortunate women they marry? Why can't they see their responsibility to their own country?'

'What Tommy means is that people shouldn't be making pilgrimages to the monastery at all,' said Spike dryly. 'He thinks they should be making pilgrimages to him. He lights candles to himself every night – all because he doesn't beat his wife. Good luck to you now, and don't let him make you miss your train with his old guff.'

Spike and the passenger shook hands, and after that Spike put him out of his head completely. Meeting strangers like that, every day of the week, he couldn't remember the half of them. But three evenings later he was waiting in the car outside the station, hoping to pick up a fare from the four-fifteen, when Mick Hurley came flopping out to him with his spectacles down his nose.

'What am I going to do with them bags you left on Tuesday, Spike?' he asked.

What was he to do with the bags? Spike looked at him without comprehension. 'What bags, Mick?'

'Them bags for Canada.'

'Holy God!' exclaimed Spike, getting slowly out of the car. 'Do you mean he forgot his bags?'

'Forgot them?' Mick Hurley repeated indignantly. 'He never travelled at all, man.'

'Holy God!' repeated Spike. 'And the liner gone since yesterday! That's a nice state of affairs.'

'Why?' asked Mick. 'Who was it?'

'A man from the monastery.'

'One of Father Felix's drunks?'

'What the hell would a drunk be coming from Canada for?' asked Spike in exasperation.

'You'd never know,' said Mick. 'Where did you leave him?'

'Over in Tommy Hanagan's bar.'

'Then we'd better ask Tommy.'

Hanagan came out to them in his shirtsleeves, his cuffs rolled up and his hat well back.

'Tommy,' said Spike, 'you remember that passenger I left in your place on Tuesday?'

Tommy's eyes narrowed. 'The big, grey-haired bloke?' he said. 'What about him?'

'Mick Hurley, here, says he never took that train. You wouldn't know what happened him?'

Tommy rested one bare, powerful arm against the jamb of the door, leaned his head against it, and delicately tilted the hat forward over his eyes. 'That sounds bad,' he said. 'You're sure he didn't go off unknown to you?'

'How could he, man?' asked Mick excitedly, feeling that some slight on the railway company was implied. 'His bags are still there. No one but locals travelled on that train.'

'The man had a lot of money on him,' Hanagan said, looking at the ground.

'You're sure of that, Tommy?' Spike asked, in alarm. It was bad enough for a motor-driver to be mixed up in a mysterious disappearance without a murder coming into it as well.

'Up to a hundred pounds,' Hanagan said, giving a sharp glance up the street. 'I saw it when he paid for the drinks. I noticed Linehan, of the guards, going in to his dinner. We might as well go over and ask him did he hear anything.'

They strode briskly in the direction of the policeman's house. Linehan came shuffling out, buttoning up his tunic – a fat, black-haired man who looked like something out of a butcher's shop.

'I didn't hear a word of it,' he said, looking from one to another, as though they might be concealing evidence. 'We'll ring up a few of the local stations. Some of them might have word of him.'

Hanagan went to get his coat. Mick Hurley had to leave them, to look after the four-fifteen, and at last Spike, Hanagan, and Linehan went to the police station, where the others waited while Linehan had long, confidential chats about football and the weather with other policemen for ten miles around. Guards are lonely souls; they cannot trust their nearest and dearest, and can communicate only with one another, like mountaineers with signal fires. Hanagan sat on the table, pretending to read a paper, though every look and gesture betrayed impatience and disgust. Spike just sat, reflecting mournfully on the loss of his good time and money.

'We'll have to find out what his name was,' Linehan said, at last. 'The best thing we can do is drive up to the monastery and get more particulars.'

'The devil fly away with Mick Hurley!' Spike said bitterly. 'Wouldn't you think he'd tell us what happened without waiting three days? If he was after losing an express train, he'd wait a week to see would it turn up.'

The three of them got into Spike's car, and he drove off up the mountain road, wondering how he was to get his fare out of it and from whom. The monks were holy enough, but they expected you to run a car on holy water, and a policeman thought he was doing you a favour if he was seen in the car with you. The veiled sunlight went out; they ran into thick mist, and before they reached the mountain-top, it had turned to rain. They could see it driving in for miles from the sea. The lights were on in the chapel; there was some service on. Spike noticed the Yank pause under the traceried window and look away down the valley. Within the church, the choir wailed, '*Et exspecto resurrectionem mortuorum. Et vitam venturi saeculi.*'

Father Felix came out and beckoned them in from the rain. His face was very grave. 'You needn't tell me what you came about, lads,' he said.

'You knew he was missing so, Father?' said Linehan.

'We saw him,' said the priest.

'Where, Father?' asked Spike.

'Out there,' Father Felix said, with a nod.

'On the mountain?'

'I dare say he's there still.'

'But what is he doing?'

'Oh, nothing. Nothing only staring. Staring at the monastery and the monks working in the fields. Poor fellow! Poor fellow!'

'But who is it?'

'One of our own men. One of the old monks. He's here these fifteen years.'

'Fifteen years!' exclaimed Linehan. 'But what came over him after all that time?'

'Some nervous trouble, I suppose,' said Father Felix in the tone of a healthy man who has heard of nerves as a well-recognized ailment of quite respectable people. 'A sort of mental blackout, I heard them saying. He wouldn't know where he'd be for a few minutes at a time.'

'Ah, poor soul! Poor soul!' sighed Linehan, with a similar blankness of expression.

'But what was taking him to Canada?' asked Hanagan.

'Ah, well, we had to send him somewhere he wouldn't be known,' explained Father Felix sadly. 'He wanted to settle down in his own place in Kilkenny, but, of course, he couldn't.'

'Why not?' asked Hanagan.

'Oh, he couldn't, he couldn't,' Linehan said, with a sharp intake of breath as he strode to the window. 'Not after leaving the monastery. 'Twould cause terrible scandal.'

'That's why I hope you can get him away quietly,' Father

Felix said. 'We did everything we could for him. Now the less talk there is, the better.'

'In that bleddy mist you might be searching the mountain for a week,' sighed Linehan, who had often shot it. 'If we knew where to look itself! We'll go up the road and see would any of Sullivan's boys have word of him.'

Sullivan's was the nearest farmhouse. The three men got into the car again and drove slowly down under the trees past the monastery. There was an iron railing, which seemed strangely out of place, and then a field, and then the bare mountain again. It was coming on to dark, and it struck Spike that they would find no one that night. He was sorry for that poor devil, and could not get over the casualness of Mick Hurley. A stationmaster! God, wouldn't you think he'd have some sense?

'It isn't Mick Hurley I blame at all,' Hanagan said angrily.

'Ah, well, Tommy, you can't be too hard on the poor monks,' Linehan said reasonably. 'I suppose they were hoping he'd go away and not cause any scandal.'

'A poor bloody loony!' snapped the Yank, his emotion bringing out a strong Boston accent. 'Gahd, you wouldn't do it to a dawg!'

'How sure you are he was a loony!' Spike said, with a sneer. 'He didn't seem so very loony to me.'

'But you heard what Father Felix said!' Hanagan cried. 'Mental blackouts. That poor devil is somewhere out on that goddam mountain with his memory gone.'

'Ah, I'll believe all I hear when I eat all I get,' Spike said in the same tone.

It wasn't that he really disbelieved in the blackouts so much as that he had trained himself to take things lightly, and the Yank was getting on his nerves. At that moment he spotted the passenger out of the corner of his eye. The rain seemed to have caught him somewhere on top of a peak, and he was running, looking for shelter, from rock to rock.

Without looking round, Spike stopped the car quietly and lit a cigarette.

'Don't turn round now, boys!' he said. 'He's just over there on our right.'

'What do you think we should do, Spike?' Linehan asked.

'Get out of the car quietly and break up, so that we can come round him from different directions,' said Spike.

'Then you'd scare him properly,' said Hanagan. 'Let me go and talk to him!'

Before they could hinder him, he was out of the car and running up the slope from the road. Spike swore. He knew if the monk took to his heels now, they might never catch him. Hanagan shouted and the monk halted, stared, then walked towards him.

'It looks as if he might come quietly,' said Linehan. He and Spike followed Hanagan slowly.

Hanagan stopped on a little hillock, hatless, his hands in his trouser pockets. The monk came up to him. He, too, was hatless; his raincoat was covered with mud; and he wore what looked like a week's growth of beard. He had a sullen, frightened look, like an old dog called to heel after doing something wrong.

'That's a bad evening now,' Hanagan said, with an awkward smile, which made him look unexpectedly boyish.

'I hope you're not taking all this trouble for me,' the monk said, looking first at Hanagan, then at Spike and the policeman, who stood a little apart from him.

'Ah, what trouble?' Hanagan said, with fictitious lightness. 'We were afraid you might be caught in the mist. 'It's bad enough even for those that know the mountain. You'd want to get those wet things off you quick.'

'I suppose so,' the monk said, looking down at his drenched clothes as though he were seeing them for the first time. Spike could now believe in the mental blackout, the man looked so stunned, like a sleepwalker.

'We'll stop at the pub and Spike can bring over whatever bags you want,' said Hanagan.

The public-house hotel looked uncannily bright after the loneliness of the mountain. Hanagan was at his most obnoxiously efficient. Linehan wanted to take a statement from the monk, but Hanagan stopped him. 'Is it a man in that state? How could he give you a statement?' He rushed in and out, his hat on the back of his head, producing hot whiskeys for them all, sending Spike to the station for the bag, and driving his wife and the maid mad seeing that there was hot water and shaving tackle in the bathroom and that a hot meal was prepared.

When the monk came down, shaved and in dry clothes, Hanagan sat opposite him, his legs spread and his hands on his thighs.

'What you'll do,' he said, with a commanding air, 'is rest here for a couple of days.'

'No, thanks,' the monk said, shaking his head.

'It won't cost you anything,' Hanagan said, with a smile.

'It's not that,' said the monk in a low voice. 'I'd better get away from this.'

'But you can't, man. You'll have to see about getting your tickets changed. We can see to that for you. You might get pneumonia after being out so long.'

'I'll have to go on,' the monk said stubbornly. 'I have to get away.'

'You mean you're afraid you might do the same thing again?' Hanagan said in a disappointed tone. 'Maybe you're right. Though what anyone wants to go back to that place for beats me.'

'What do people want to go back anywhere for?' the monk asked in a dull tone.

Spike thought it was as close as he'd ever seen anyone get to knocking the Yank off his perch. Hanagan grew red, then rose and went in the direction of the door, suddenly changed his mind, and turned to grasp the monk's left hand in his own two. 'I'm a good one to talk,' he said in a thick voice. 'Eighteen years, and never a day without thinking of this place. You mightn't believe it, but there were nights I cried myself to sleep. And for what, I ask you? What did I expect?'

He had changed suddenly; no longer the big-hearted, officious ward boss looking after someone in trouble, he had become humble and almost deferential. When they were leaving, he half opened the front door and halted. 'You're sure you won't stay?' he snapped over his shoulder.

'Sure,' said the monk, with a nod.

Hanagan waved his left arm, and they went out across the dark square to the station.

Spike and he saw the last of the monk, who waved to them till the train disappeared in the darkness. Hanagan followed it, waving, with a mawkish smile, as though he were seeing off a girl. Spike could see that he was deeply moved, but what it was all about was beyond him. Spike had never stood on the deck of a liner and watched his fatherland drop away behind him. He didn't know the sort of hurt it can leave in a boy's mind, a hurt that doesn't heal even when you try to conjure away the pain by returning. Nor did he realize, as Hanagan did at that moment, that there are other fatherlands, whose loss can hurt even more deeply.

(1954)

THE MASS ISLAND

WHEN Father Jackson drove up to the curates' house, it was already drawing on to dusk, the early dusk of late December. The curates' house was a red-brick building on a terrace at one side of the ugly church in Asragh. Father Hamilton seemed to have been waiting for him and opened the front door himself, looking white and strained. He was a tall young man with a long, melancholy face that you would have taken for weak till you noticed the cut of the jaw.

'Oh, come in, Jim,' he said with his mournful smile. ' 'Tisn't much of a welcome we have for you, God knows. I suppose you'd like to see poor Jerry before the undertaker comes.'

'I might as well,' Father Jackson replied briskly. There was nothing melancholy about Jackson, but he affected an air of surprise and shock. ' 'Twas very sudden, wasn't it?'

'Well, it was and it wasn't, Jim,' Father Hamilton said, closing the front door behind him. 'He was going downhill since he got the first heart attack, and he wouldn't look after himself. Sure, you know yourself what he was like.'

Jackson knew. Father Fogarty and himself had been friends, of a sort, for years. An impractical man, excitable and vehement, Fogarty could have lived for twenty years with his ailment, but instead of that, he allowed himself to become depressed and indifferent. If he couldn't live as he had always lived, he would prefer not to live at all.

They went upstairs and into the bedroom where he was.

The character was still plain on the stern, dead face, though, drained of vitality, it had the look of a studio portrait. That bone structure was something you'd have picked out of a thousand faces as Irish, with its odd impression of bluntness and asymmetry, its jutting brow and craggy chin, and the snub nose that looked as though it had probably been broken twenty years before in a public-house row.

When they came downstairs again, Father Hamilton produced half a bottle of whiskey.

'Not for me, thanks,' Jackson said hastily. 'Unless you have a drop of sherry there?'

'Well, there is some Burgundy,' Father Hamilton said. 'I don't know is it any good, though.'

'Twill do me fine,' Jackson replied cheerfully, reflecting that Ireland was the country where nobody knew whether Burgundy was good or not. 'You're coming with us tomorrow, I suppose?'

'Well, the way it is, Jim,' Father Hamilton replied, 'I'm afraid neither of us is going. You see, they're burying poor Jerry here.'

'They're what?' Jackson asked incredulously.

'Now, I didn't know for sure when I rang you, Jim, but that's what the brother decided, and that's what Father Hanafey decided as well.'

'But he told you he wanted to be buried on the Mass Island, didn't he?'

'He told everybody, Jim,' Father Hamilton replied with growing excitement and emotion. 'That was the sort he was. If he told one, he told five hundred. Only a half an hour ago I had a girl on the telephone from the Island, asking when they could expect us. You see, the old parish priest of the place let Jerry mark out the grave for himself, and they want to know should they open it. But now the old parish priest is dead as well, and, of course, Jerry left nothing in writing.'

'Didn't he leave a will, even?' Jackson asked in surprise.

'Well, he did and he didn't, Jim,' Father Hamilton said, looking as if he were on the point of tears. 'Actually, he did make a will about five or six years ago, and he gave it to Clancy, the other curate, but Clancy went off on the Foreign Mission and God alone knows where he is now. After that, Jerry never bothered his head about it. I mean, you have to admit the man had nothing to leave. Every damn thing he had he gave away — even the old car, after he got the first attack. If there was any loose cash around, I suppose the brother has that.'

Jackson sipped his Burgundy, which was even more Australian than he had feared, and wondered at his own irritation. He had been irritated enough before that, with the prospect of two days' motoring in the middle of winter, and a night in a godforsaken pub in the mountains, a hundred and fifty miles away at the other side of Ireland. There, in one of the lakes, was an island where in Cromwell's time, before the causeway and the little oratory were built, Mass was said in secret, and it was here that Father Fogarty had wanted to be buried. It struck Jackson as sheer sentimentality; it wasn't even as if it was Fogarty's native place. Jackson had once allowed Fogarty to lure him there, and had hated every moment of it. It wasn't only the discomfort of the public-house, where meals erupted at any hour of the day or night as the spirit took the proprietor, or the rain that kept them confined to the cold dining- and sitting-room that looked out on the gloomy mountainside, with its couple of whitewashed cabins on the shore of the lake. It was the over-intimacy of it all, and this was the thing that Father Fogarty apparently loved. He liked to stand in his shirt-sleeves behind the bar, taking turns with the proprietor, who was one of his many friends, serving big pints of porter to rough mountainy men, or to sit in their cottages, shaking in all his fat whenever they told broad stories or sang risky folk songs. 'God, Jim, isn't it grand?' he would say in his deep voice, and Jackson would look at him over his spectacles with what Fogarty called his 'Jesuitical look', and say, 'Well, I suppose it all depends on what you really like, Jerry.' He wasn't even certain that the locals cared for Father Fogarty's intimacy; on the contrary, he had a strong impression that they much preferred their own reserved old parish priest, whom they never saw except twice a year, when he came up the valley to collect his dues. That had made Jackson twice as stiff. And yet now when he found out that the plans that had meant so much inconvenience to him had fallen through, he was as disappointed as though they had been his own.

'Oh, well,' he said with a shrug that was intended to conceal his perturbation, 'I suppose it doesn't make much difference where they chuck us when our time comes.'

'The point is, it mattered to Jerry, Jim,' Father Hamilton said with his curious shy obstinacy. 'God knows, it's not anything that will ever worry me, but it haunted him, and somehow, you know, I don't feel it's right to flout a dead man's wishes.'

'Oh, I know, I know,' Jackson said lightly, 'I suppose I'd better talk to old Hanafey about it. Knowing I'm a friend of the Bishop's he might pay more attention to me.'

'He might, Jim,' Father Hamilton replied sadly, looking away over Jackson's head. 'As you say, knowing you're a friend of the Bishop's, he might. But I wouldn't depend too much on it. I talked to him till I was black in the face, and all I got out of him was the law and the rubrics. It's the brother Hanafey is afraid of. You'll see him this evening, and, between ourselves, he's a tough customer. Of course, himself and Jerry never had much to say to one another, and he'd be the last man in the world that Jerry would talk to about his funeral, so now he doesn't want the expense and inconvenience. You wouldn't blame him, of course. I'd probably be the same myself. By the way,' Father Hamilton added, lowering his voice, 'Before he does come, I'd like you to take a look round Jerry's room and see is there any little memento you'd care to have – a photo or a book or anything.'

They went into Father Fogarty's sitting-room, and Jackson looked at it with a new interest. He knew of old the rather handsome library – Fogarty had been a man of many enthusiasms, though none of long duration – the picture of the Virgin and Child in Irish country costume over the mantelpiece, which some of his colleagues had thought irreverent, and the couple of fine old prints. There was a newer picture that Jackson had not seen – a charcoal drawing of the Crucifixion from a fifteenth-century Irish tomb, which was brutal but impressive.

'Good Lord,' Jackson exclaimed with a sudden feeling of loss. 'He really had taste, hadn't he?'

'He had, Jim,' Father Hamilton said, sticking his long nose into the picture. 'This goes to a young couple called Keneally, outside the town, that he was fond of. I think they were very kind to him. Since he had the attack, he was pretty lonely, I'd say.'

'Oh, aren't we all, attack or no attack,' Jackson said almost irritably.

Father Hanafey, the parish priest of Asragh, was a round, red, cherubic-looking old man with a bald head and big round glasses. His house was on the same terrace as the curates'. He, too, insisted on producing the whiskey Jackson so heartily detested, when the two priests came in to consult him, but Jackson had decided that this time diplomacy required he should show proper appreciation of the dreadful stuff. He felt sure he was going to be very sick next day. He affected great astonishment at the quality of Father Hanafey's whiskey, and first the old parish priest grew shy, like a schoolgirl whose good looks are being praised, then he looked self-satisfied, and finally he became almost emotional. It was a great pleasure, he said, to meet a young priest with a proper understanding of whiskey. Priests no longer seemed to have the same taste, and as far as most of

them were concerned, they might as well be drinking po-
teen. It was only when it was seven years old that Irish
began to be interesting, and that was when you had to catch
it and store it in sherry casks to draw off what remained of
crude alcohol in it, and give it that beautiful roundness that
Father Jackson had spotted. But it shouldn't be kept too
long, for somewhere along the line the spirit of a whiskey
was broken. At ten, or maybe twelve, years old it was just
right. But people were losing their palates. He solemnly as-
sured the two priests that of every dozen clerics who came
to his house not more than one would realize what he was
drinking. Poor Hamilton grew red and began to stutter, but
the parish priest's reproofs were not directed at him.

'It isn't you I'm talking about, Father Hamilton, but
elderly priests, parish priests, and even canons, that you
would think would know better, and I give you my word, I
put the two whiskeys side by side in front of them, the shop
stuff and my own, and they could not tell the difference.'

But though the priest was mollified by Father Jackson's
maturity of judgement, he was not prepared to interfere in
the arrangements of the funeral of his curate. 'It is the wish
of the next-of-kin, Father,' he said stubbornly, 'and that is
something I have no control over. Now that you tell me the
same thing as Father Hamilton, I accept it that this was
Father Fogarty's wish, and a man's wishes regarding his own
interment are always to be respected. I assure you, if I had
even one line in Father Fogarty's writing to go on, I would
wait for no man's advice. I would take the responsibility on
myself. Something on paper, Father, is all I want.'

'On the other hand, Father,' Jackson said mildly, drawing
on his pipe, 'if Father Fogarty was the sort to leave written
instructions, he'd hardly be the sort to leave such unusual
ones. I mean, after all, it isn't even the family burying
ground, is it?'

'Well, now, that is true, Father,' replied the parish priest
and it was clear that he had been deeply impressed by this

rather doubtful logic. 'You have a very good point there, and it is one I did not think of myself, and I have given the matter a great deal of thought. You might mention it to his brother. Father Fogarty, God rest him, was *not* a usual type of man. I think you might even go so far as to say that he was a rather *unusual* type of man, and not orderly, as you say – not by any means orderly. I would certainly mention that to the brother and see what he says.'

But the brother was not at all impressed by Father Jackson's argument when he turned up at the church in Asragh that evening. He was a good-looking man with a weak and pleasant face and a cold shrewdness in his eyes that had been lacking in his brother's.

'But why, Father?' he asked, turning to Father Hanafey. 'I'm a busy man, and I'm being asked to leave my business for a couple of days in the middle of winter, and for what? That is all I ask. What use is it?'

'It is only out of respect for the wishes of the deceased, Mr Fogarty,' said Father Hanafey, who clearly was a little bit afraid of him.

'And where did he express those wishes?' the brother asked. 'I'm his only living relative, and it is queer he would not mention a thing like that to me.'

'He mentioned it to Father Jackson and Father Hamilton.'

'But when, Father?' Mr Fogarty asked. 'You knew Father Jerry, and he was always expressing wishes about something. He was an excitable sort of man, God rest him, and the thing he'd say today might not be the thing he'd say tomorrow. After all, after close on forty years, I think I have the right to say I knew him,' he added with a triumphant air that left the two young priests without a leg to stand on.

Over bacon and eggs in the curates' house, Father Hamilton was very despondent. 'Well, I suppose we did what we could, Jim,' he said.

'I'm not too sure of that,' Jackson said with his 'Jesuitical air', looking at Father Hamilton sidewise over his spectacles. 'I'm wondering if we couldn't do something with that family you say he intended the drawing for.'

'The Keneallys,' said Father Hamilton in a worried voice. 'Actually, I saw the wife in the church this evening. You might have noticed her crying.'

'Don't you think we should see if they have anything in writing?'

'Well, if they have, it would be about the picture,' said Father Hamilton. 'How I know about it is she came to me at the time to ask if I couldn't do something for him. Poor man, he was crying himself that day, according to what she told me.'

'Oh dear!' Jackson said politely, but his mind was elsewhere. 'I'm not really interested in knowing what would be in a letter like that. It's none of my business. But I would like to make sure that they haven't something in writing. What did Hanafey call it – "something on paper"?'

'I dare say we should inquire, anyway,' said Father Hamilton, and after supper they drove out to the Keneallys', a typical small red-brick villa with a decent garden in front. The family also was eating bacon and eggs, and Jackson shuddered when they asked him to join them. Keneally himself, a tall, gaunt, cadaverous man, poured out more whiskey for them, and again Jackson felt he must make a formal attempt to drink it. At the same time, he thought he saw what attraction the house had for Father Fogarty. Keneally was tough and with no suggestion of lay servility towards the priesthood, and his wife was beautiful and scatterbrained, and talked to herself, the cat, and the children simultaneously. 'Rosaleen!' she cried determinedly. 'Out! Out I say! I told you if you didn't stop meowing you'd have to go out . . . Angela Keneally, the stick! . . . You do not want to go to the bathroom, Angela. It's only five minutes since you were there before. I will not let Father Hamilton come up to you at all unless you go to bed at once.'

In the children's bedroom, Jackson gave a finger to a stolid-looking infant, who instantly stuffed it into his mouth and began to chew it, apparently under the impression that he would be bound to reach sugar at last.

Later, they sat over their drinks in the sitting-room, only interrupted by Angela Keneally, in a fever of curiosity, dropping in every five minutes to ask for a biscuit or a glass of water.

'You see, Father Fogarty left no will,' Jackson explained to Keneally. 'Consequently, he'll be buried here tomorrow unless something turns up. I suppose he told you where he wanted to be buried?'

'On the Island? Twenty times, if he told us once. I thought he took it too far. Didn't you, Father?'

'And me not to be able to go!' Mrs Keneally said, beginning to cry. 'Isn't it awful, Father?'

'He didn't leave anything in writing with you?' He saw in Keneally's eyes that the letter was really only about the picture, and raised a warning hand. 'Mind, if he did, I don't want to know what's in it! In fact, it would be highly improper for anyone to be told before the parish priest and the next-of-kin were consulted. All I do want to know is whether' – he waited a moment to see that Keneally was following him – 'he did leave any written instructions, of any kind, with you.'

Mrs Keneally, drying her tears, suddenly broke into rapid speech. 'Sure, that was the day poor Father Jerry was so down in himself because we were his friends and he had nothing to leave us, and—'

'Shut up, woman!' her husband shouted with a glare at her, and then Jackson saw him purse his lips in quiet amusement. He was a man after Jackson's heart. 'As you say, Father, we have a letter from him.'

'Addressed to anybody in particular?'

'Yes, to the parish priest, to be delivered after his death.'

'Did he use those words?' Jackson asked, touched in spite of himself.

'Those very words.'

'God help us!' said Father Hamilton.

'But you had not time to deliver it?'

'I only heard of Father Fogarty's death when I got in. Esther was at the church, of course.'

'And you're a bit tired, so you wouldn't want to walk all the way over to the presbytery with it. I take it that, in the normal way, you'd post it.'

'But the post would be gone,' Keneally said with a secret smile. 'So that Father Hanafey wouldn't get it until maybe the day after tomorrow. That's what you were afraid of, Father, isn't it?'

'I see we understand one another, Mr Keneally,' Jackson said politely.

'You wouldn't, of course, wish to say anything that wasn't strictly true,' said Keneally, who was clearly enjoying himself enormously, though his wife had not the faintest idea of what was afoot. 'So perhaps it would be better if the letter was posted now, and not after you leave the house.'

'Fine!' said Jackson, and Keneally nodded and went out. When he returned, a few minutes later, the priest rose to go.

'I'll see you at the Mass tomorrow,' Keneally said. 'Good luck, now.'

Jackson felt they'd probably need it. But when Father Hanafey met them in the hall, with the wet snow falling outside, and they explained about the letter, his mood had clearly changed. Jackson's logic might have worked some sort of spell on him, or perhaps it was just that he felt they were three clergymen opposed to a layman.

'It was very unforeseen of Mr Keneally not to have brought that letter to me at once,' he grumbled, 'but I must say I was expecting something of the sort. It would have been very peculiar if Father Fogarty had left no instructions at all for me, and I see that we can't just sit round and wait to find out what they were, since the burial is tomorrow. Under the circumstances, Father, I think we'd be justified in arranging for the funeral according to Father Fogarty's known wishes.'

'Thanks be to God,' Father Hamilton murmured as he and Father Jackson returned to the curates' house. 'I never thought we'd get away with that.'

'We haven't got away with it yet,' said Jackson. 'And even if we do get away with it, the real trouble will be later.'

All the arrangements had still to be made. When Mr Fogarty was informed, he slammed down the receiver without comment. Then a phone call had to be made to a police station twelve miles from the Island, and the police sergeant promised to send a man out on a bicycle to have the grave opened. Then the local parish priest and several old friends had to be informed, and a notice inserted in the nearest daily. As Jackson said wearily, romantic men always left their more worldly friends to carry out their romantic intentions.

The scene at the curates' house next morning after Mass scared even Jackson. While the hearse and the funeral car waited in front of the door, Mr Fogarty sat, white with anger, and let the priests talk. To Jackson's surprise, Father Hanafey put up a stern fight for Father Fogarty's wishes.

'You have to realize, Mr Fogarty, that to a priest like your brother the Mass is a very solemn thing indeed, and a place where the poor people had to fly in the Penal Days to hear Mass would be one of particular sanctity.'

'Father Hanafey,' said Mr Fogarty in a cold, even tone, 'I am a simple businessman, and I have no time for sentiment.'

'I would not go so far as to call the veneration for sanctified ground mere sentiment, Mr Fogarty,' the old priest said severely. 'At any rate, it is now clear that Father Fo-garty left instructions to be delivered to me after his death, and if those instructions are what we think them, I would have a serious responsibility for not having paid attention to them.'

'I do not think that letter is anything of the kind, Father Hanafey,' said Mr Fogarty. 'That's a matter I'm going to inquire into when I get back, and if it turns out to be a hoax, I am going to take it further.'

'Oh, Mr Fogarty, I'm sure it's not a hoax,' said the parish priest, with a shocked air, but Mr Fogarty was not con-vinced.

'For everybody's sake, we'll hope not,' he said grimly.

The funeral procession set off. Mr Fogarty sat in the front of the car by the driver, sulking. Jackson and Hamilton sat behind and opened their breviaries. When they stopped at a hotel for lunch, Mr Fogarty said he was not hungry and stayed outside in the cold. And when he did get hungry and came into the dining-room, the priests drifted into the lounge to wait for him. They both realized that he might prove a dangerous enemy.

Then, as they drove on in the dusk, they saw the moun-tain country ahead of them in a cold, watery light, a light that seemed to fall dead from the ragged edge of a cloud. The towns and villages they passed through were dirtier and more derelict. They drew up at a crossroads, behind the hearse, and heard someone talking to the driver of the hearse. Then a car fell into line behind them. 'Someone join-ing us,' Father Hamilton said, but Mr Fogarty, lost in his own dream of martyrdom, did not reply. Half a dozen times within the next twenty minutes, the same thing happened, though sometimes the cars were waiting in lanes and by-roads with their lights on, and each time Jackson saw a heavily coated figure standing in the roadway shouting to the hearse driver: 'Is it Father Fogarty ye have there?' At last they came to a village where the local parish priest's car was waiting outside the church, with a little group about it. Their headlights caught a public-house, isolated at the other side of the street, glaring with whitewash, while about it was the vague space of a distant mountainside.

Suddenly Mr Fogarty spoke. 'He seems to have been fairly well known,' he said with something approaching politeness.

The road went on, with a noisy stream at the right-hand side of it falling from group to group of rocks. They left it for a by-road, which bent to the right heading towards the stream, and then began to mount, broken by ledges of naked rock, over which hearse and cars seemed to heave themselves like animals. On the left-hand side of the road was a little whitewashed cottage, all lit up, with a big turf fire burning in the open hearth and an oil lamp with an orange glow on the wall above it. There was a man standing by the door, and as they approached he began to pick his way over the rocks towards them, carrying a lantern. Only then did Jackson notice the other lanterns and flashlights, coming down the mountain or crossing the stream, and realize that they represented people, young men and girls and an occasional sturdy old man, all moving in the direction of the Mass Island. Suddenly it hit him, almost like a blow. He told himself not to be a fool, that this was no more than the desire for novelty one should expect to find in out-of-the-way places, mixed perhaps with vanity. It was all that, of course, and he knew it, but he knew, too, it was something more. He had thought when he was here with Fogarty that those people had not respected Fogarty as they respected him and the local parish priest, but he knew that for him, or even for their own parish priest, they would never turn out in midwinter, across the treacherous mountain bogs and wicked rocks. He and the parish priest would never earn more from the people of the mountains than respect; what they gave to the fat, unclerical young man who had served them with pints in the bar and egged them on to tell their old stories and bullied and ragged and even fought them was something infinitely greater.

The funeral procession stopped in a lane that ran along the edge of a lake. The surface of the lake was rough, and they could hear the splash of the water upon the stones. The two priests got out of the car and began to vest themselves, and then Mr Fogarty got out, too. He was very nervous and hesitant.

'It's very inconvenient, and all the rest of it,' he said, 'but I don't want you gentlemen to think that I didn't know you were acting from the best motives.'

'That's very kind of you, Mr Fogarty,' Jackson said. 'Maybe we made mistakes as well.'

'Thank you, Father Jackson,' Mr Fogarty said, and held out his hand. The two priests shook hands with him and he went off, raising his hat.

'Well, that's one trouble over,' Father Hamilton said wryly as an old man plunged through the mud towards the car.

'Lights is what we're looking for!' he shouted. 'Let ye turn her sidewise, and throw the headlights on the causeway the way we'll see what we're doing.'

Their driver swore, but he reversed and turned the front of the car till it almost faced the lake. Then he turned on his headlights. Somewhere farther up the road the parish priest's car did the same. One by one, the ranked headlights blazed up, and at every moment the scene before them grew more vivid – the gateway and the stile, and beyond it the causeway that ran towards the little brown stone oratory with its mock Romanesque doorway. As the lights strengthened and steadied, the whole island became like a vast piece of theatre scenery cut out against the gloomy wall of the mountain with the tiny whitewashed cottages at its base. Far above, caught in a stray flash of moonlight, Jackson saw the snow on its summit. 'I'll be after you,' he said to Father Hamilton, and watched him, a little perturbed and looking behind him, join the parish priest by the gate. Jackson resented being seen by them because he was weeping, and he was a man who despised tears – his own and others'. It was like a miracle, and Father Jackson didn't really believe in miracles. Standing back by the fence to let the last of the mourners pass, he saw the coffin, like gold in the brilliant light, and heard the steadying voices of the four huge mountainy men who carried it. He saw it sway above the heads, shawled and bare, glittering between the little stunted holly bushes and hazels.

(1959)

Walter Macken

One of Ireland's greatest novelists

The Bogman £1.50

Tricked into marriage to the sexless, middle-aged Julia, Cahal's heart
is lost to the wanton Maire, and his rebellion grows ...

Brown Lord of the Mountain 90p

Donn Donnschleibhe returns to his home village, bringing new life,
marvellous changes — and revenge ...'

The Coll Doll and other stories 90p

Twenty-two stories of birth, love, death; of people happy and sad —
publicans, poets, children, tinkers, snobs and sweethearts ...

Rain on the Wind 1.25

A rich, racy story of the fisherfolk of Galway; of fighting and
drinking, of hurling and poaching, of weddings and wakes.

Frank O'Connor

The Mad Lomasneys and other stories 80p

'Brilliant and penetrating studies of young men who are either agin
the government or agin religion, young women who have a struggle
between their good Catholic consciences and sex, or priests who
have to struggle with both' OXFORD MAIL

Lewis Grassic Gibbon
A Scots Quair £2.95

From the years of the Great War to the hungry thirties, Lewis Grassic Gibbon's magnificent trilogy spans the life of a woman and the story of a people. This powerful saga of Scottish life through three decades is now published in one volume.

'His three great novels have the impetus and music of mountain burns in full spate' OBSERVER

Jean Stubbs
The Ironmaster £1.75

Three children were born to Ned and Dorcas Howarth of Kit's Hill, high on the Pennines. Charlotte, strong-willed wife of a London radical, was robbed of her man by death and brought back to Kit's Hill. Sturdy Dick, born to inherit his father's farm, would wait for the good and golden harvest that never comes. But bright young William, now master of his own forge, had his eyes fixed on the future: in the dawn of industrial England, he was the Howarth destined for greatness, a man born to be ironmaster.

Wilkie Collins
The Woman in White £1.95

'A solitary woman, dressed from head to foot in white garments ...'

From the moment of Walter Hartright's strange encounter on a moonlit Hampstead Heath, the reader is caught up in the spell of Wilkie Collins' gripping narrative and driven on to the end of a novel that stands as one of the greatest mystery thrillers in the language.

Fiction

☐	**Options**	Freda Bright	£1.50p
☐	**The Thirty-nine Steps**	John Buchan	£1.25p
☐	**Secret of Blackoaks**	Ashley Carter	£1.50p
☐	**A Night of Gaiety**	Barbara Cartland	90p
☐	**The Sittaford Mystery**	Agatha Christie	£1.00p
☐	**Dupe**	Liza Cody	£1.25p
☐	**Lovers and Gamblers**	Jackie Collins	£2.25p
☐	**Sphinx**	Robin Cook	£1.25p
☐	**Ragtime**	E. L. Doctorow	£1.50p
☐	**Rebecca**	Daphne du Maurier	£1.75p
☐	**Flashman**	George Macdonald Fraser	£1.50p
☐	**The Moneychangers**	Arthur Hailey	£1.95p
☐	**Secrets**	Unity Hall	£1.50p
☐	**The Maltese Falcon**	Dashiell Hammett	95p
☐	**Simon the Coldheart**	Georgette Heyer	95p
☐	**The Eagle Has Landed**	Jack Higgins	£1.75p
☐	**The Master Sniper**	Stephen Hunter	£1.50p
☐	**Smiley's People**	John le Carré	£1.75p
☐	**To Kill a Mockingbird**	Harper Lee	£1.50p
☐	**The Empty Hours**	Ed McBain	£1.25p
☐	**Gone with the Wind**	Margaret Mitchell	£2.95p
☐	**The Totem**	Tony Morrell	£1.25p
☐	**Platinum Logic**	Tony Parsons	£1.75p
☐	**Rage of Angels**	Sidney Sheldon	£1.75p
☐	**The Unborn**	David Shobin	£1.50p
☐	**A Town Like Alice**	Nevile Shute	£1.50p
☐	**A Falcon Flies**	Wilbur Smith	£1.95p
☐	**The Deep Well at Noon**	Jessica Stirling	£1.75p
☐	**The Ironmaster**	Jean Stubbs	£1.75p
☐	**The Music Makers**	E. V. Thompson	£1.50p

Non-fiction

☐	**Extraterrestrial Civilizations**	Isaac Asimov	£1.50p
☐	**Pregnancy**	Gordon Bourne	£2.95p
☐	**Out of Practice**	Rob Buckman	95p
☐	**The 35mm Photographer's Handbook**	Julian Calder and John Garrett	£5.95p
☐	**Travellers' Britain**	} Arthur Eperon	£2.95p
☐	**Travellers' Italy**		£2.95p
☐	**The Complete Calorie Counter**	Eileen Fowler	70p

☐	**The Diary of Anne Frank**	Anne Frank	£1.25p
☐	**Linda Goodman's Sun Signs**	Linda Goodman	£1.95p
☐	**Mountbatten**	Richard Hough	£1.95p
☐	**How to be a Gifted Parent**	David Lewis	£1.95p
☐	**Symptoms**	Sigmund Stephen Miller	£2.50p
☐	**Book of Worries**	Robert Morley	£1.50p
☐	**The Hangover Handbook**	David Outerbridge	£1.25p
☐	**The Alternative Holiday Catalogue**	edited by Harriet Peacock	£1.95p
☐	**The Pan Book of Card Games**	Hubert Phillips	£1.50p
☐	**Food for All the Family**	Magnus Pyke	£1.50p
☐	**Everything Your Doctor Would Tell You If He Had the Time**	Claire Rayner	£4.95p
☐	**Just Off for the Weekend**	John Slater	£2.50p
☐	**An Unfinished History of the World**	Hugh Thomas	£3.95p
☐	**The Third Wave**	Alvin Toffler	£1.95p
☐	**The Flier's Handbook**		£5.95p

All these books are available at your local bookshop or newsagent, or can be ordered direct from the publisher. Indicate the number of copies required and fill in the form below

....

Name..
(Block letters please)

Address...

....

Send to Pan Books (CS Department), Cavaye Place, London SW10 9PG
Please enclose remittance to the value of the cover price plus:
35p for the first book plus 15p per copy for each additional book ordered
to a maximum charge of £1.25 to cover postage and packing
Applicable only in the UK

While every effort is made to keep prices low, it is sometimes
necessary to increase prices at short notice. Pan Books reserve
the right to show on covers and charge new retail prices which
may differ from those advertised in the text or elsewhere